Andy dug his he
inadequately maske
the bag when she smoothly rose off him. He
clutched at her, and through her legs he could see
a similar female figure crouched over Jim. Before
he could absorb what was happening she had turned
lithely and was crouching over his head. The warm
damp musk covered his nose and as his tongue
licked out he found that his oral digit too was
sucked into her demanding channel. It was like
kissing a particularly skillful, beautifully tasting
mouth, he thought in a moment of sanity. The
warm cavern of her mouth had descended on his
shaft and engulfed it. Sharp little teeth were teasing
the bottom side of the erect maleness, and her lips
and tongue sucked demandingly at him. Thought
was impossible as waves of pleasure caused his
frame to tremble and jerk. His balls contracted
spasmodically. For the first time in his life Andy
felt the actual progress of his sperm through the
channel of his cock. His tongue and cock both
held prisoner, both struggling to imprison themselves
deeper, he spurted semen into her welcoming mouth,
his hips arcing wildly off the floor.

## *Other books by Blue Moon Authors*

### *RICHARD MANTON*

**DREAM BOAT**
**LA VIE PARISIENNE**
**SWEET DREAMS**
**LOVE LESSONS**
**BELLE SAUVAGE**
**PEARLS OF THE ORIENT**
**BOMBAY BOUND**

### *DANIEL VIAN*

**BLUE TANGO**
**SABINE**
**CAROUSEL**
**ADAGIO**
**BERLIN 1923**

### *AKAHIGE NAMBAN*

**CHRYSANTHEMUM, ROSE, AND THE SAMURAI**
**SHOGUN'S AGENTS**
**WOMEN OF THE MOUNTAIN**
**WARRIORS OF THE TOWN**
**WOMEN OF GION**

**BLUE MOON BOOKS**
**61 Fourth Avenue**
**New York, New York 10003**

# *Masters of*

# CLOUDS

## *and*

# RAIN

*Anonymous*

BLUE MOON BOOKS, INC. NEW YORK

First Blue Moon Edition 1990
First Printing 1990

ISBN 0-929654-78-1

Manufactured in the United States of America.

Published by Blue Moon Books, Inc.
61 Fourth Avenue
New York, New York 10003

# CHAPTER 1:
# PROLOG

Sitting in his favorite bar, Jim Suzuki contemplated his whisky glumly. The weather had something to do with his mood. The soft night was falling unnoticed onto Tokyo's garish streets. There was a hint of spring in the air, brought as a trace over the heavy fumes of exhausts, cooking, and humanity. He needed space and some natural quiet to relax in. It was not that his work was strenuous, and he enjoyed it in any case. He was a more-than-competent systems analyst, though formally a student. But with the hint of spring in the air, being cooped up in front of a glowing screen had somehow lost its attraction. Moreover, he had a problem, one that needed careful thinking out.

The door to Sato's tiny bar blew open admitting the fumes of the street. Someone sat down next to Jim but he barely raised his head. The symptom of Jim Suzuki's problem spoke.

"I thought I'd find you in here."

"Yeah," Jim answered. As if sensing the mood, Sato-san, the ex-wrestler barman brought a warmed ceramic bottle of sake. The bottle was poured, the tiny cup sipped at, and Jim heard a familiar breath of satisfaction. He turned around and looked at his own face. His twin brother stared back, then drained his tiny *sakazuki* again.

"Want to talk about it?" Andy Middler inquired.

"I guess we better."

Sato watched both faces covertly. The two men, one seemingly a foreigner, the other apparently Japanese had been coming into his bar on a regular basis for several months. What drew the barkeep's gaze was the similarity between the faces. The major differences had to do with obvious physical features: the Japanese one of the pair had almond eyes, sallower skin, smooth black hair. The other had rounder eyes and brown curly hair. Discounting those superficial differences, the two faces were like two peas in a pod and Sato shivered, thinking of dark magic.

"Mary Typhon. That one-night stand of her's sure put us to a lot of trouble."

Andy grinned. "Yeah, Mom dear Mom. Now don't go sentimental on me. I hope she was one hell of a lay. That's not the point. Our daddies are the problem." They drank in silence. They knew they were freaks of nature: twins, born of a single egg and two separate spermatozoa. The odds against it boggled the mind, but nonetheless, there they were.

"Still want to find our daddies?" Andy asked.

"I guess we better. In any case, I need a break, and its now between terms." Formally, at least, Jim was a student working for his Ph.D. "Lets review the facts. Two men, one Japanese the other American. We know that one, at least, who presumably is your father, Andy, is Leonard Fine, ex-US Navy. My father: unknown. Second, both of us have been supported for many years by funds originat-

ing from a Japanese company. Third, the company headquarters and ownership are somewhere in the Kiso area:
the Japan Alps. Okay so far?''

"Yeah." Andy took up the tale. "And someone named
Kitamura Dansuke, the boss of the Clouds and Rain Corporation, whatever that is, is either after our hides for
some reason, or just doesn't want us poking into things."
Andy spoke while looking at his cup, then beckoned to
the bartender who was attending to another drinker. The
small bar was beginning to fill up.

"And fifth," Jim said, grabbing for the full bottle Sato-
san had placed before Andy and filling his own whisky
glass. Andy automatically held out his tiny cup and Jim
filled it to the brim as well. "Someone, perhaps this very
same Kitamura, is leading us a merry dance, dangling
clues in front of our eyes and snatching them away again.
Mysterious, what? He he he.''

They drank to the Shadow.

"I'll tell you what," Andy muttered. "Let's get drunk
tonight, then track those two horny bastards to their lair."

"Onwards to Kiso!" They drank again and this time
Jim ordered a whisky for each of them. Andy, who was
usually more cautious in his drinking eyed the glass doubtfully, but did not protest.

"You are American?" A hesitant Japanese voice broke
into their drinking. A rather plump business type in horn
rimmed glasses and three piece suit stood beside them
diffidently. They nodded together. "You rike *osake*'?"

"Very much." Andy was being polite, though Jim only
scowled.

The plump man made motions to the barman and all
three of them were soon ensconced before some more sake
bottles. Even Jim began to thaw, particularly when Matsu-

mura-san paid their tab without question and hustled them off good naturedly to "very nice prace. Rots of girrs."

They waved goodnight to Sato-san and Matsumura led them in the direction of the Roppongi entertainment district. He tried his atrocious English on them, roaring with laughter at his own mistakes and telling them about his own business and love life with a frankness that would have shocked anyone not familiar with the Japanese. Andy, who had had the experience of being hosted by a genial semi-drunk Japanese businessman out for a demonstration lesson in English before, was thoroughly enjoying himself. The man was obviously loaded, wanted nothing more than to be able to boast to his business associates about his foreign friends (to wit, Jim and himself), and Andy was ready to indulge him. Jim, some of his drunkenness disappearing in the taxi ride, was somewhat more reserved. There was something odd about the man, whether it was his linguistic mistakes which seemed too patterned, or the sharp glances he shot at the twins when he thought they were not looking.

The bar he took them to was a members' club. Situated in the top floor of a building in Roppongi it was a conscious imitation of the American Playboy clubs. Deep velour seats were served by leggy young waitresses in panda suits, complete with short skirts, net stockings, and white and black masks with round fuzzy ears.

Matsumura ordered drinks and small *otsumami* snacks as they sat down. He tried to fondle one of the waitresses' legs, and she gracefully moved out of reach. Soon they were joined by three hostesses. They were dressed in long gowns, slit all the way up the thigh. They lit Matsumura's cigarettes, chattered incessantly and flirted with the men.

"Ah, I forgot," Matsumura said owlishly. He reached for the inner pocket of his jacket and pulled out his *meishi* case. Jim and Andy automatically did the same. They exchanged cards and the two Americans examined Matsumura's cursorily. All it indicated was that he represented a company called WHEELS, which meant nothing to either brother.

"I want one, too!" pouted the hostess who was stroking Andy's knee. She was a small round thing. Her full, red painted lips were ideal for pouting and she made the most of it. Her face reminded Andy of Natsumi, a girl who insisted on teasing him before allowing him into her. He handed her his card and Jim did the same. Matsumura was obviously well enough known and he ignored the request, calling loudly for drinks.

"What is your name?" Andy asked. "Takako," she said and giggled. "You like?"

He nodded. "But you have no *meishi* card. You had better give me something instead."

"But I have nothing to give you!" she said in mock horror.

"I'll just take yourself then . . ."

She giggled again and hid her mouth with her palm. "No. But I'll give you . . . this." and she unpinned a small cheap brooch that kept the top of her dress closed. Andy peered lecherously down her cleavage, noting she wore nothing to hide her breasts under the dress, and she giggled again.

The drinks arrived. *Mizuwari* for Matsumura, neat whisky for Jim, sake for Andy. The three girls pretended to drink from tall highball glasses of soda water.

They discussed their mutual businesses, though Jim and Andy comparing notes later agreed that Matsumura really said little enough about himself. The evening seemed to pass in a haze of alcohol. They fondled the hostesses as much as those allowed, talked, ate little snacks. Near midnight the two brothers rose unsteadily to their feet. Matsu-mura rose, too, obviously almost too drunk to move. He laughed uproariously as his hostess supported him His eyes focused on the floor. Deliberately and carefully like any drunk he bent slowly down and picked up a sheet of old fashioned thick Japanese paper.

"This is yours, I think," he said in a stage whisper. He smiled broadly and handed it to Jim. The smile did not seem to reach his eyes. Jim blearily took the paper and shoved it into his jacket pocket, then headed unsteadily to the door, assisted by Shizu, the small-breasted middle-aged woman who was his hostess. The girls insisted on accompanying them down the elevator. Jim amorously squeezed Shizu's full, tight bum and she pecked his cheek. Andy tried squeezing Takako's breasts and she giggled again as he hefted them, then pushed him away with a laugh as the elevator reached ground level. They stepped out and the girls bowed them off, then disappeared into the elevator.

Once back home, Jim staggered to the couch and col-lapsed. "I'm getting too old for those drinking bouts," he moaned.

Andy, only slightly less drunk, laughed at him. "Hot coffee?"

"Hell no. Bed. What the hell's this?' He fumbled in his jacket pocket and withdrew the folded square of Japa-nese paper.

"Billet doux, eh? From your lovely lady. . . ." Andy staggered into the kitchen. "Andy! Come here!" He replaced the coffeepot and returned to the living room. Jim wordlessly handed him the paper. Its grey, rather rough surface was printed with an old fashioned trades-man's bill. On it was stamped ACCOUNT CLOSED in red. In handwriting someone had added "Mr. Kitamura would appreciate closing the matter. Either way."

They looked at the note silently.

"I think . . ." Andy started, then swallowed.

". . . we've just been threatened." His brother concluded the sentence for him. Still puzzled, they went to bed, not before checking the doors and windows carefully: several weeks before two *yakuza* types had broken in, apparently to threaten them, but been dissuaded by a very active friend of theirs.

Andy groaned and reached for the phone. The sun shone cheerfully through the window and Andy glared at it. He looked at his watch: ten.

"Harro? Moshi moshi, Middlaa-san?"

He perked up. The voice was unfamiliar, but a female voice in the morning . . .

"Yes, this is Andy Middler."

"You remember me? I am Takako. From club? . . ." she let her sentence trail off.

"Of course I remember," Andy said heartily, the fog beginning to dissipate. "Your lovely calling card is right before me . . ."

She giggled. "Is not calling card. It is very valuable personal jewelry . . ." Giggling again.

"Then I must return it to you."

"Oh no. It was a gift. Maybe you give me something else?"

"I'd love to. Where can I meet you?"

"You are at home? Yes? I will come. Do you know where Mr. Suzuki is? Maybe he would like to see Shizu-san again? I bring her?"

"Of course," said Andy. "Mr. Suzuki, Jim, lives here with me. We are related," he said without elaboration.

He gave her directions, then staggered out of bed to wake Jim.

Jim peered at him and grimaced. "Now what do you need two hookers for?"

"Hookers? You mean," the paler brother spluttered. "You mean . . ."

"You think they were after your beautiful body you sap?"

"Never thought of it. Thought you could find them only in massage parlors."

Jim fluttered his fingers. "These are a higher grade. Choose their customers themselves. What the hell. I can afford it this week."

"I can't," Andy said gloomily.

Jim punched his brother's shoulder. "Come on J.P. Morgan. I'll pay for the broads, you pay for the drinks."

The two women stood at the door of the modest apartment and peered in expectantly. Andy smiled broadly and opened the door to its fullest extent.

"Please come up," he indicated the interior and the two twittered their way into the apartment. Jim turned to them from the small table he had been busy at, and handed each a delicate porcelain sake cup.

"It is too early to drink, but still cold outside . . ."

The two women peeked at their glasses as Jim handed Andy his own drink. Steam rose from the little cups. The liquid inside was bright red.

"Mulled wine," Jim answered their unspoken question. They seated themselves, Shizu and Andy on the sofa, Jim and Takako in armchairs. They sipped.

"Delicious!" the older woman exclaimed in surprise. She crossed her legs, showing an expanse of white stockinged thigh.

Takako nodded hasty agreement, and Jim poured her a

second tiny cup over her objections. They discussed the club, and the two men gradually brought the conversation over to their host of the previous night.

Matsumura, it turned out, had been a regular visitor to the club for precisely one week. Long enough to establish himself as a regular, with a bar bill. He spent well, and beyond that no one really cared what he did or whom he was.

Jim looked at Andy and shrugged his eyebrows. There was obviously nothing to be discovered there. And in any case, there were other matters on his mind. Shizu's small plump hand was describing circles on his knee. Her face was lowered and he could not see her expression. Takako on the other hand was smiling gaily at Jim. Jim looked at his brother and jerked his head casually. Andy recalled the etiquette Jim had drilled into him.

"You have been so kind to come. There is something we want to give you." He leaned towards the small lamp stand beside the sofa and handed one of the two packages there to Jim, then turned to Shizu.

"I must pin it on myself . . ."

For a moment the woman's features bore a look of alarm. She was not quite sure the *gaijin* knew what was expected from him. Jim untied the red and gold threads that closed the bulky little envelope and extracted the thick faience Moroccan bead Jim had found among his things. Rolled inside the opening were several 10,000 yen bills. She smiled and bent her head when he whispered in her ear, "I think I must put this on myself."

He turned to her and held her face in his hands while slipping the thread over her head. His hands stroked the length of her face then he followed the thread to the opening of her one piece dress. "It really should be worn inside, close to your skin," he whispered, and his fingers slipped between the lapels, skillfully undoing the large buttons. His palms flattened on her small breasts and he could feel the tiny erect nipples harden at his touch. Her mouth was suddenly on his and he felt her hands searching at his crotch and releasing his tumescence from the confines of his pants. Her tongue explored his and she leaned forward, pressing herself against his hands while she twisted her torso to face him more fully.

Jim received the small parcel and weighed it in his hands while grinning at Takako. He extracted the bead slowly, watching Andy and Shizu out of the corner of his eye. Takako's eyes widened at the roll of bills tucked into the bead.

"This is a good-luck bead," he whispered, his attention partly on Andy who had his hands inside Shizu's dress as the older woman squirmed around to accommodate him. "I must put it in the safest place possible."

She nodded bright eyed, and Jim rose from his seat and crouched beside her, then raised one stockinged foot. The nylon slid through his hands as he slipped the bead string over it. She raised her leg. Her loose skirt fell back on her thighs and Jim placed her firm rather thick calf on his shoulder. Her nylon-covered thigh was exposed to his gaze. Beneath the layers of nylon and lace he could see the dark shadow of her hair. His nostrils were teased by the warm female scent of her as he slid questing fingers down the warm thigh until the bead rested against the slightly moist, warm mound of her cunt. He bunched his fingers and pulled at the fabric.

"That will not do, it will not do at all. For the best effect, it must be touching the skin."

Obligingly she raised her ass to permit him to pull off her pants.

Andy was breathing heavily. His cock was fully out of

his pants and Shizu was straddling him, her dress fully undone. Under it she wore nothing but the sheer white panty hose. He nibbled at her shoulder, then at her soft tits and thickening nubbins of her nipples while she unbuttoned his shirt, running expert hands over his chest. Her moist tongue penetrated his ear, then she raised herself from his lap. Bending over she pulled down her white tights. Andy, taking advantage of her position, guided her willing mouth to his erect cock. Willingly she sucked it in while crouching to divest herself of the flimsy material. He clutched at her breast, elongated by her position, then she straightened and motioned him to rise. She quickly stripped him, stood back a moment to admire his full red-tipped manhood, then turned to walk towards the door leading to the bedrooms. Andy hastily followed, one hand clutching firmly at her solid bottom, the other fondling her small breasts and roving over her full belly.

Jim watched them go with regret. He would have liked to watch as his brother fucked the woman. He turned back to Takako instead. She rose with him and he led her towards his own room. Her nylons and lacy panties remained puddled on the floor. One of his hands and one of hers were joined between her thighs, supporting the bead at the moist entrance to her cunt.

She lay back on the couch, her legs spread wide. Jim ran his index finger along the lips of her cunt. Her bottom moved in slow sensuous circles on the bed. He added a second finger and she joined him, then raised her own finger to her lips and licked the musky fluid off. He added a third and forth finger and speeded up the movements of his hand. Her eyes remained fixed on the young man as she stroked the inner lips of her cunt, rubbing her nails against his churning digits and collecting as much of her dew as she could. Before she could raise the hand to her mouth Jim had captured it with his lips. He sucked the taste of her cunt from her fingers.

Takako hooked her fingers under Jim's chin and pulled him forward. He felt between her thighs, his rampant cock searching out the warm, flowing slit. Takako raised her hips to facilitate his entry then locked her heels over his back. He shafted in and out of her, urged on by her cries and by the feel of her nails on his back.

"Feel my behind," she begged. Jim obeyed, exploring her plump rear, clutching the generous mounds.

"Now my tits." His head descended to one prominent nipple, and she guided his hand to the other.

"Squeeze them!"

He squeezed the prominent buttery mounds, then set off to explore her body with his hands as she urged him on wordlessly with twitches of her body. His movements became wilder, less controlled and the long shaft shuttled into her frothing cunt, covering their bellies with moisture. A tremor overtook him and he shuddered violently in her as a spurt of fluid ejected from his balls and flooded her interior. Takako smiled at him, pulled his mouth to hers and she explored his mouth with her tongue while he emptied himself into her.

At last he made a move to extricate himself from her embrace.

"Not yet," she whispered. "There is still much left in you." She began working the muscles of her thighs and cunt, gradually working his embedded cock into standing order.

Andy peered up at Shizu, excited afresh by the liquid sounds of love from the other room. She straddled his thighs, his cock jutting forward through her black pubic hairs. White streaks of his semen clustered on the hairs and shaft, and yet he was still erect. She slid her plump belly back and forth along the shaft. The rough slickness of the hairs excited him again to action. He raised his hands and played with her rather flat breasts, then clutched at her small ass, trying to raise her for penetration. Obligingly she rose to a squat over him. He held her ass while she pointed the rampant male member at her waiting opening. Her cunt lips were rather long and she took great pleasure in showing them off, teasing the reluctant-seeming opening with the broad cock-head. Then she sank down gradually, examining his expression intently. When he was fully embedded in her she started a rough jogging motion. Andy looked between her legs and she obligingly spread the lips of her cunt, parting the hairs so that he should have a complete look at his shaft. The dark lips parted reluctantly as she rose, greedily gulping the shaft as she descended. He liked the tenseness of the muscles in the inner part of her thighs.

Gradually Andy lost interest in the visual sensations as the impact of the tactile ones grew. He started heaving his hips up off the mattress, slamming himself deeply into the plump woman above him. She ground her hips in pestle-like movements over his loins, scratching at his chest as she did so. His own hands were roving over her body now, seeking out the pleasure of her skin.

As the crisis started to overtake him Shizu bent forward. She rubbed her nipples against his excited chest, then clamped her mouth over his. Her mouth explored and conquered his tongue as the first spurts of semen left his cock. He jerked into her again and again, supported at times only by his heels and shoulders. Crouched over him, a glorious dark jockey, she urged him on as she consumed his mouth.

Andy fell back on the bed. Shizu raised herself and peered into his eyes. With a deliberate motion she took his hand in hers. She slid their hands over her body, down the crease between her buns, past the tiny bud of her ass hole. His shaft was still embedded in her, and the flesh and hair around the opening were covered with his discharges. She collected those on the tips of her fingers. With a slow deliberate motion she raised her hand to her face and sucked his fluids into her red-painted mouth. Andy looked on as a final tiny twitch shook his frame once again.

The two young men considered their options once Shizu and Takako had left. They were both thinking of Matsumura and his implied warning.

"Someone is going to a lot of trouble. . . ." Jim said thoughtfully.

"Maybe we should drop it all?" Andy thought out loud. Jim merely looked at him as he continued, "No. The hell with it. Let's get it on. Onward to Kiso."

# CHAPTER 2:

# RAIN ON THE SPAIN

"Are you sure spring is here?" Jim asked grumpily, trying to shed the water from his collar.

Andy shivered, but did not reply.

They had decided to start the journey by hitchhiking, and had soon learned to regret the decision. The skies that had been a clear blue as they left Tokyo were now leaden grey. The rain fell in a steady drizzle, and the only time that stopped was when it came down in sheets.

"To hell with it, it's dark already. Let's get something to eat, somewhere to stay, and a bus tomorrow, or a train."

They looked around. The narrow highway, just off the expressway where hitchhiking was forbidden, looked gloomily deserted. The occasional cars ignored them.

"There's a fluorescent light down the way."

Jim peered through the rain, sneezed, and grunted assent. "Where there's a fluorescent, there's life. And maybe a *koheeshoppu* where we can get some food."

They trudged wearily through the downpour. The light

was disappointing—merely an ad for a cosmetic, but beyond it they could see a mock stucco front with the hoped for sign KOHEESHOPPU: SUPAIN it said in Japanese *kana* characters. They heaved a sigh of relief, hoisted their packs, and walked in. The place was deserted. Dusty bottles of Spanish wine, wooden furniture, posters of bullfights tried to create an ambience that the dark wet outside and the very Japanese smells and sights managed to dispel.

"*Gomen kudasai!*" they called out together.

There was a faint shout from the back and a patter of feet.

A thin young woman, her hair falling down her back, her plain house dress casually draped on her made an appearance from the door to the back. "*Irasshaimase,*" she called out automatically, though there was obvious puzzlement and surprise in her glance. "I'm sorry, we're closed . . ." she started to say, then noted the blue *noren* curtain still hanging over the entrance. "Oh. I forgot again." She looked at the two bedraggled visitors and her pinched expression softened. "I'll get you something?"

"Please," Andy said, suppressing a sneeze. "Coffee and something hot to eat. Anything as long as it's hot."

"*Paera*" she said automatically. "It's sort of like a *piraff,* you know rice cooked with vegetables. . . ."

The two nodded in unison as she bustled about. "I must get the *noren* off though," she laughed suddenly. "I'm new to this business. My husband drives a truck and he's away. I don't really know what to do."

She sat by them and chattered while they gratefully gulped the steaming rice. Without waiting for them to ask, she served second helpings of steaming food and coffee.

"Why Spain?" Andy broke into her monologue about the difficulties of life in the small town.

"My husband and I. We want to go to Spain. So warm,

and the music, the people . . ." there was a dreamy look in her eyes that betrayed some long-held emotion. Her thin rather hard face softened, became almost beautiful.

"Is there an inn or hotel around here?" Andy asked.

She started to answer when Jim spotted a guitar hanging on the wall. "May I?" he asked, reaching for it.

She nodded, ignoring Andy's question, her eyes on Jim who was handling the instrument, running his fingers across the strings, tightening a peg. He began strumming it, inexpertly playing a Spanish sounding rhythm. Gradually his fingers recalled the movements and he started singing "La Llorona," an old Pete Seeger favorite in a low voice.

She listened entranced as he finished "Llorona," and started playing another song. Neither his inexpert handling of the instrument nor his unmusical voice which he purposely pitched low detracted from her pleasure. He finished, made a face, and sucked the tips of his left-hand fingers.

Andy repeated his question.

Her eyes still on Jim, she muttered a negative.

"Damn. You hear Jim?"

"What?" asked his brother still trying out half-forgotten chords.

"No place to sleep, dummy. And it's raining outside."

Jim started playing again.

"You can stay here," she said abstractedly. "Though you will have to leave early in the morning . . ." her hands were clasped before her breast, lost in images of Andalusia.

Jim started singing again. It was some sad pseudo-Spanish love song he had learned years ago in Germany of all places. Tears of sadness or pleasure rolled down her thin cheeks. The look on her face aroused Andy. He stroked her hair gently. She turned her body towards him, her face still rapt with Jim's playing. Jim lowered his eyelids, suiting his expression to the song. Andy could barely suppress his laughter at the bathos, and his hands kept on stroking her. He rose and sat beside her on the large wooden chair. She allowed him to stroke her body, feel her breasts. She wore no bra and he could feel the soft flesh of her breast through the armhole of her dress. Pressing his advantage, he whispered wordlessly in her ears as Jim sang on. His hands, emboldened, roved freely over her body and she rested her flank against him, nestling into the warmth of his body.

Jim grinned inwardly and went down to one knee without stopping his strumming. He rested his head for a moment in her lap. Her dress had risen above her bare knee and he kissed it delicately. The guitar slipped from his hands and his lips covered her knees and the insides of her thighs with little kisses. The hem rose to expose her panties. She lay back against Andy's chest, allowing the two men to explore her while bathetic tears flowed down her cheeks. Then she pushed both men gently away and rose to her feet. She led them, her hands in theirs, their other hands busy with her hips and buttocks, to an inner room. It was filled by an "old fashioned" brass bed covered with a colorful quilt. She dimmed the light and dropped her dress and panties and gracefully slid under the crisp white sheets. Jim and Andy followed with alacrity, nestling on either side of her.

She turned to face Andy. His knee was soon between her thighs and she could feel his erect prick against her belly. Her skin quivered at the touch. His mouth covered hers. Behind her, in the wide bed, she felt Jim stroke her tight behind. He insinuated a hand along the crack and she squirmed. Andy raised her thigh over his and felt with one hand for her moist slit. She had little hair on her mound and her lips were fluid with her inner juices. Andy tried to bend his cock down to her entrance as her hands went around his neck. He longed to turn her over on her back and plunge into her, but Jim's urgency, he knew, would be as great as his own. Instead he wriggled further down the bed until the tip of his cock was nuzzling at the head of her slit. Grasping the shaft, ignoring the rest of her body, he began stroking the teary one-eyed tip against her willing vulva.

"Aha aha," she gasped brokenly, fondling behind her with one hand while her other cradled Andy's head. He tried to kiss her but she avoided his mouth, burying her face in her arm. At last he found sufficient leverage and with a groan of pleasure felt his silken shaft sinking deeply into her willing flesh.

Their bellies were pushed close together and Andy, attempting to help Jim find release stroked the girl's ass, then pulled the mound upward. She ahhhd again and started jogging forward on his willing prick.

"Faster," she demanded, her head still buried in her arm. He stroked as fast as he could, the head slipping out from inside the moist channel, pushed in again by the sheer force of their mutual urgency.

With his left hand Andy tried stroking her shoulder but it was too short to reach her breast. Jim's hand insinuated itself between their two bodies and he squeezed the taut delightful mound. With his other hand Jim was trying to direct his cock at her rear opening, at the opening already occupied by his brother, at anything at all. But her strong hand kept him away as she rode his brother's prick. Defeated, Jim stopped butting at her ass with his cock and waited his turn. He held her body loosely and squeezed at her breasts, feeling Andy's chest with the back of his hands. As if in reward for his patience she began milking his rampant shaft with her free hand.

Jim moved his attention to the center of the action. His hand drifted down towards the juncture of the two sweating bodies. She encouraged him, sucking in her soft belly to allow his hand access. He nibbled at her neck as he stroked her clitoris, mashed between Andy's pistoning rod and her own pubis. She yowled again, and her head began tossing from side to side as her climax approached. A small shudder shook her frame and Andy's cock, slick with her juices suddenly was coated with gobs of sperm that ran off the shaft and onto Jim's fingers. Jim stroked her ass again and tried to moisten her tiny rear entrance with Andy's copious flow.

"Stop it!" she said in a stern voice, pinching his cock roughly. Jim desisted and Andy, aware of the other young man's needs, pulled reluctantly out of the warm tube. She squirmed over to face Jim and crammed his waiting cock into her overflowing cunt. The slipperiness of her insides was enhanced by Andy's copious discharge. Jim's cock glided up her spermaceous channel to the hilt and she grunted in satisfaction. He kissed her neck roughly and she urged him on with her hands on his butt. Andy stroked her shoulders and neck, rubbing his softened cock against her buttocks as Jim rammed into her with a will. He rolled her onto her back and pounded away at her, his face set. Andy aided his brother's motions, pinching at the woman's nipples, stroking her flanks, finally raising her heels above Jim's bobbing ass.

"Huh, uh. Huh, uh," she grunted wildly.

"Mi amor, mi amor," Jim encouraged her. She cried out wildly in response, thrusting back up at him, biting his shoulder. He clasped her thin buttocks, kneading the mounds of flesh and balancing himself on her pubis. The wave of orgasm washed over both of them together and their pubes jammed together in a sodden hairy tangle.

Jim collapsed on her and lay silently until she pushed him off. The two men nestled on either side. She stroked their cocks idly and they fell asleep to the sound of her contented humming.

# CHAPTER 3:

# THINGS GO BETTER

"You know, I actually know someone in this town," Jim said musingly when they reached Gifu City.

"Is he likely to be a good host?" Andy asked.

"Probably." He grinned suddenly. "I helped him lose his virginity, or at least I think I did."

"Do tell, young man, do tell . . ."

They had descended from the bus that had carried them through a rainy countryside deeper into the mountains of central Japan. The train would have been easier, but their final hitchhiking stop the previous day had left them no option but the bus. Besides, all they knew was that somewhere within the mountains was the headquarters of the Clouds and Rain Company. May McCormick, whose husband was in the cosmetic business and had told them about the company, had not been able to supply much detail. Nor had any other of their friends. Taking local buses seemed a logical, and cheap, way of spying out the countryside. And though the rain had dampened their spirits somewhat, this was still a holiday. Deep inside himself,

Andy admitted he did not really care if they ever found the objective of their search. It was simply good to be away from the city, away from his work as a financial analyst, away from everything.

"Nakabe was with me at university. He went back home a few months ago to run his parents' electronic store. About six months ago we played majong. He had a girlfriend with him, . . ."

"Oh yeah, I know the rest. All three of you screwed her."

"Damn straight," Jim said, his face lighting reminiscently.

"You're going to cream in your pants if you keep on looking like that, Bro."

A female voice answered the phone *"Moshi moshi?"*

"This is Suzuki Jim. May I speak to Mr. Nakabe?"

"Jim-san? Jim-san is that you? This is Chieko . . ." Her voice stumbled a bit. "I am Mrs. Nakabe now."

"Wonderful for you, Nakabe-san," Jim chuckled. "You are well, I hope?"

"Where are you?" she asked. There was a peculiar warmth in her tone, not that of an almost-newly married bride, but of a woman speaking to her first lover. Which Jim had in point of fact been.

"I'm here on a trip and I thought I'd visit Nakabe."

"Yes, of course. He is at the office, but I will buzz him. Jim-san, it is wonderful to hear from you again."

Nakabe was effusive when he met Jim and Andy. It was obvious that he enjoyed his success and he showed them around the three floor electronics store with a great deal of pride. The clerks were duly impressed by the boss's foreign friends, and even more impressed when Jim, on a whim, helped them solve a software problem while Andy, Nakabe, and his wife talked investments and business. Andy covertly studied the woman. She was obviously edgy, expectantly looking up as if hoping Jim would appear from his labor on the computers at any minute. She was thin and intense, her eyes residing in deep hollows, her hair piled on her head. She dressed modestly but with care, a heavy ring on one finger the major attestation of her husband's wealth. Under the jittery exterior, however, Andy found a sharp mind well versed in the practical economics of her family's business.

Nakabe himself was an intense young man, suitably impressed by the gravity and elevation of his own position. He was brusque and imperious with his clerks and salesmen, but behind the rather gross exterior Andy could detect flashes of economic intelligence that seemed to indicate he would go far. They fell easily into an easy familiarity based on their mutual interest in financial affairs.

Jim reappeared, his dark hair tousled. He grinned at them. "Solved it!" He looked at his watch. "It's getting late, we had better go . . ."

"Nonsense!" Nakabe said. "You will come to dinner with us. Mountain greens. It's just the beginning of the season and the shoots are so tender. Then we'll go drinking." Chieko Nakabe lowered her eyes, and there was an impression of calculation when she raised her head to her husband.

"Let's go to the Leopard later," she said.

Nakabe looked at her in some confusion. It was obvious she had not been expected to come with them. Then he grinned at the unconventionality of it and grunted agreement.

Much later they found themselves in the plush environs of a cocktail lounge. Over small plates of tidbits and overpriced whiskey they listened to an indifferent pianist, joined later by an electronic combo that set Jim's teeth on edge, and the two guests looked around curiously at the people who flowed in and out of what was an obviously popular drinking spot. Over their heads the stuffed head of the leopard that gave the place its name snarled impartially at everyone.

The din was incredible for such a place and the cigarette haze obscured all but one's immediate surroundings. Andy and Nakabe were deep into a discussion of the mechanics of small business expansion punctuated by anecdotes and stories when Chieko leaned forward and spoke to Jim.

"Do you still fancy me?" she said bluntly. Her eyes were on her husband who was telling Andy a story. The story was obviously a sexy one, because Nakabe was keeping his voice low and showing Andy a gesture with his hands. The band continued playing raucously in the background.

"Actually, I do," Jim confessed, watching his brother and Nakabe talk. "Can you get out tonight?"

"I can, but I won't. I want you to do something for me."

"What?" he asked, his charcoal eyebrows rising. Chieko seemed to have attained a brittle sharpness that he did not remember from their previous encounter. Married life was either agreeing with her, or was extremely disagreeable. He thought he might ask her at some point. But not now.

"Do you see that girl in the corner? In that group of young people? Isn't she beautiful?" she asked irrelevantly.

Jim looked in the indicated direction. The girl was plump without being fat. High breasts rode a compact square-shouldered body. She laughed fully, showing pearly white teeth that contrasted pleasingly with a red-painted mouth and shoulder-length black hair. "Yes," he said. "Quite pretty."

"She's beautiful," said Chieko. There was a peculiar tremor in her voice. "Do you think you could seduce her?"

The question caught him by surprise. "I imagine so, if I put my mind to it. Yes, why not. But why do you want me to do that?"

"I love her," Chieko said, peering into her glass. "I saw her first at my wedding night, and I fell in love." She gripped Jim's arm. "You must help me get her. You can do what you want with me, but I must have her."

He was baffled "Why don't you try to seduce her yourself?" he asked.

"I've tried. I've tried, but I don't know how to do it with a girl. And I lose my head every time I'm near her." Her nails dug into his arm and she stared at the happy group in the corner.

"Hey," Nakabe called to them. "Let's go to another place. I know a place where they serve wonderful *oden* stew and good sake . . ." He was drunk and owlish, his rounded face red with drink.

Jim laughed."Nakabe-san, you could always drink me under the table. I think I need to go to bed. . . ."

Chieko looked on disapprovingly but her husband ignored her.

"Nonsense, nonsense, Jim-san. Let's have some fun."

Andy picked up the cue Jim had thrown him with a slight motion of his fingers. "Come on, Nakabe-san. Let's leave this weakling to go to the hotel and sleep. I'm with you." He laughed hoarsely and threw his arm around the other man's shoulder. They staggered off, laughing, into the night.

"I'm not going to be around long!" Jim warned Chieko when the other two left. "Andy and I are in the middle of a project. We have to leave tomorrow."

"Come back," she begged, turning her eyes to him. "You must help me . . . !"

"Something on account then," he said cruelly. His hand slid under the table and he felt her nylon covered leg. "I'll do it. But I haven't had a woman for some time. After you've introduced us," he saw the look of rebellion on her face and continued. "Yes, after you've introduced us. In any case, I have no chance with her on such a short notice. Then you go out and meet me in the alley beside the bar."

"This is Saga Mineko," Chieko said gaily after she had dragged the other girl from the group of young people she had been sitting with. She smiled shyly as he introduced himself, rose, and bowed. Not used to that sort of courtesy, she looked up at him, wide-eyed under heavy lashes. Jim had had an opportunity to examine her as she approached. She was good looking, Jim had to admit, and there was a hint of unawakened sultriness beneath her maidenly exterior that he longed to arouse. He poured her a drink without a word, and she sat demurely by his side as they made conversation. He flattered her choice of clothes and the beauty of the town, and she responded with shy animation.

"I forgot!" he said suddenly. "Here, have my calling card." It was his most impressive one, the one with the computer company he was president of: $200, registered in California. Mineko's eyes widened.

"I'm sorry," she said. "I have no card to give you. I work in the department store here, and of course . . ."

"No matter," Jim said expansively. "You'll be a manager some day yet."

She laughed, and Chieko laughed with her.

"No, I'm serious," Jim exclaimed. "I am a physiognomist, and I can see by the lines on your face that you will be an important person some day.''

Her heavy eyelashes eyes widened ''Really? You are able to read the face? How clever! Can you do a full reading?''

He saw she was serious, and Chieko was raptly bending to hear him as well, her hand resting lightly on the other girl's thigh. Only Jim noted the slight tremor in the thin digits.

''I can, of course,'' he said. ''But not here. These things should be private . . .''

''Oh, what a shame. I wish you were staying longer, but if you must leave tomorrow . . .''

''For such a beauty as you,'' she blushed slightly, ''I shall be forced to return.''

She smiled, her full lips widening in a pout. ''I must return to my friends,'' she said in a low voice. ''Goodbye . . .''

Jim rose with her and shook her hand. For one instant he stroked her wrist, then the length of her fingers as she withdrew from his hand. A faint spark rose to her eyes, then was gone.

He said goodnight loudly to Chieko as he stepped towards the door to the lounge. Down the stairs and into the cool night air which cleared his lungs from the fumes of tobacco and liquor. When he heard the tap of high heels on the brick steps behind him he turned and headed down the dark street, lit pallidly by the few lanterns that signalled still-open drinking places. He paused before a darkened alley, and as Chieko came up, bundled her into it.

''That was a good start, Jim-san. I am so anxious.''

Jim could feel the trembling in her thighs as he pressed against her. His own emotions were stirred by the presence of both women. He pulled her to him urgently.

She moved into his arms and he held her for a moment comfortingly. "If we stay here, someone will see us, but we can't go to the hotel or your house either." She nodded unquestioningly. Her warm breath blowing at his collar.

"You said you'd do whatever I required, right?"

She nodded again, and a shiver, of cold or pleasure, racked her.

"Well, what I need most is to be relaxed when I approach her. I'm too horny for that. . . ."

She nodded her understanding and her hand reached for his fly. The contact with his warm erect cock was expected and she started to rub the silky shaft, holding it awkwardly in an inexperienced grip.

"Not that. That's not what I want."

"I can't kneel here in the dirt!" she said furiously.

"All you have to do is bend over," Jim soothed her.

She nodded and bent down, squatting on her high heeled shoes. Her warm mouth engulfed the tip of his cock.

She was not expert, but her mouth was warm and soft. The occasional scrapes from her teeth added spice to Jim's feeling as he imagined what would happen with Mineko. He seized her coiffured head and started controlling its movements, rubbing her up and down the shaft of his prick. Then he changed his motions, holding her motionless while he explored her extended mouth with his cock as if it were a kissing tongue. He pulled the shaft out almost to the tip and rubbed it against her soft thin lips, then drove it in again to rest against the root of her tongue until he felt her beginning to gag. Her surrender to his immediate needs was total. In a moment of cruelty he grasped the broad shaft and beat her lips and cheeks gently with it. She ahhd loudly in appreciation, then sucked his cock in again and began to take an active part in the process. Her tongue licked out, laving the broad head,

dipping beneath the shelf of the broad crown. Tickling the
most sensitive spot under the tip with the broad flat of her
tongue, she loosed his balls from their confinement. At
first she held the precious sack gently in her palm, then
she angled her head and sucked each delicate egg in turn
into her hot cavernous mouth. She pushed them out with
her tongue and resumed her lingual bathing. Jim reacted
by jerking forward, the tide of his lust spilling out the tip
in preliminary bursts just before a flood churned through
the erect fleshy hose and spurted into her waiting mouth.

Shudders shook his frame and he emptied himself gratefully into her waiting mouth. She swallowed the sticky
fluids, carefully catching every drop for fear some tiny
driblet would give her away later. In her imagination she
was Mineko's vagina, filling with Jim's cock, and she was
content in the knowledge that she would be the next at
that treasure.

"How are you going to do it?" she asked as she rose,
straightening her clothes.

"I don't know yet," Jim admitted. "Is she a virgin, do
you know?"

"I think so," said Chieko thoughtfully. "We once went
to a hot spring, as a group, and she as much as admitted
she had never had a man. Some of the girls teased her.
Oh Jim, she is *so* beautiful . . ."

"Do you care if she's willing or not?" he asked
carefully.

"Don't hurt her!" Chieko said in sudden concern.

"Of course not, what do you take me for? But there
are ways which would not make her as loving as you
could wish . . ."

"That does not matter," Cheiko said firmly. "I will
make her love me, once . . . once. . . ."

Jim smiled. "Once I have done the dirty work, eh?

Well, I'll call you. Go home now. If I get her into bed tonight . . ."

"You'll call me immediately," she broke in, half demanding, half pleading.

"Yes, I'll do that. Won't Nakabe be suspicious?"

"He'll be too drunk," she said with something of a sneer.

Andy staggered slightly and only then discovered he was drunk. He wondered where Jim had gotten to. He had been so busy listening to Nakabe's stories that he had not paid any attention. And Chieko was gone, too, which meant any of several interesting possibilities. Nakabe had been sodden drunk when Andy had loaded him into a taxi and sent him home, and now he realized he hadn't the faintest idea where he was. He looked around him. The place was unfamiliar. He turned, trying to get his directions. Someone was approaching in the dark. He peered through the alcoholic haze and saw it was the figure of a young woman. She smiled at him and some of her teeth flashed silver in the light of a passing car. Andy smiled back and decided to ask her the directions to the small business hotel he and Jim were inhabiting.

"Excuse me," he said in polite Japanese, "can you tell me where I can find the Sakura Hotel?"

"Do you like sex?" she asked him in the same polite tone.

Andy gaped at her and some of the fog started to lift in a hurry. A slight drizzle misted his face. He examined her more closely. She wore an ankle length skirt and dark sweater. Her tan raincoat was open, and from what he could see in the intermittent light of passing cars, her figure was good. She bore the scrutiny patiently. A faint smile curved her darkly painted lips. She tilted her head at Andy and repeated the question.

"Do you like sex?"

Andy decided to play up to her. "Of course I do, and I'd love to have some with you." He was about to add a deprecating comment, to take the sting out of his words.

"Of course," she nodded. She stepped back into the shadow of a shuttered shop entrance. In the dark he saw she was raising her skirt. "Well, come on then!" she said urgently.

He stepped into the dark, completely stupefied. With some impatience her hand sought the fly of his jeans. He moved her hand away and unzipped himself. He saw she was holding up the folds of her skirt. His cock swung free. She spread her legs and braced her shoulders against the corner of the shop entrance. Her eyes were on him. He rubbed his cock and it rose to a proud erection. Her eyes were on him, but she turned her mouth aside as he bent to kiss her.

He reached for her crotch. Her cunt lips were slippery and wet and she gasped slightly. Her hips jerked forward. He bent his knees and guided the erect crown of his cock to the entrance. She sighed at his fumbling, then moaned with pleasure as his cock found the slippery entrance. Raising herself on her toes she guided the *gaijin* in. He was the first she had had in her midnight perambulations, and she was looking forward to it.

Andy rose, carrying her with him. He clutched at her bottom, digging his fingers into the flesh.

"Yes, yes. Fuck me. O, o, o, fuck me more. Do what you want. Fuck my cunt." She was mumbling incoherently as he rose and dropped with her riding his prick. Her legs were widely splayed in the doorway, her mouth seeking his.

"Squeeze me. My tits. My ass. My cunt . . ." she muttered at every thrust, squirming to find more contact with his flesh, with his erect cock that was piercing her so. Andy furiously ground his hips into hers. He was panting heavily, from her weight and from the efforts of his lust. His orgasm was slow in coming, and she squealed in delight as he redoubled his efforts and she herself reached peak after peak.

Finally Andy thrust forward with all his strength. His arms and legs felt like lead, pulled along by the insistent demands of his balls. His hips arched and his eyes stared unseeing. A mass of sperm spewed out of his balls, boiled along the length of his man-hose and emptied into her clutching recesses. He clenched her ass as hard as he could and she squealed with suppressed pain and delight.

As his cock softened she lowered her nylon clad leg and stood on the ground. She extracted a tissue from her small bag and wiped it between her legs. Her hand was suddenly on his shoulder, coaxing him forward. "Did you like it? Would you like some more?" She smiled brilliantly.

He nodded wordlessly.

· "Take me to you house," she whispered.

"I can't," Andy confessed. "I'm only staying the night at a hotel."

"You're leaving tomorrow?" A vertical line appeared in her brows as she thought for a moment. "Then you must come to my house. I live in an *apaato* so you must be very quiet."

They crept quietly up the outside metal stairs. He could not read the name on the door. Without turning on the light they stepped in and dropped their shoes. Her apartment was the usual *yojohan:* four and a half *tatami* mats in size. The tiny kitchen was stark. A *futon* was spread all ready for its occupant in the tiny room.

They stripped in the glow of a night light. She had a bushy flattened thatch of dark hair. Pale body supported unremarkable breasts. She stood on the *futon*, spread her legs and inserted her hand inside her cunt. Giggling, she reached for him with the other. She spoke in a nervous high pitched voice as she felt his cock.

"So large. So *gaijin* neh? You'll fuck me, won't you? Are you pink there? I can't see. Nice, thick like a Coke bottle. I want you inside me. Come on cock, come on."

Whether it was the words, uttered in her nervous monotone, or the insistent pulling at his member, Andy did not know. But sooner than he would have thought possible he was erect and ready for her. She laid herself down quickly on the *futon* and slid a cushion under her buttocks. Her hip bones and bushy mound were made prominent. Andy knelt between her legs and started stroking her pussy. It was still wet with their discharges.

"No," she said. "Come inside. Fuck me! Fuck me!"

He did as he was bid. Her insides were slick and slippery. He rode her without caring about her pleasure. She called out in a low voice, describing her own sensations, the feel of his manhood inside her, the parts of her body that she touched and fondled, pinched and squeezed without reference to him at all. Spittle appeared at the corner of her mouth. Her frame shook in orgasm, then again and again. Still Andy rode her. He tried to roll her over but she resisted, only clutching his frame to her, stroking and pinching his butt. When he tried to withdraw, bored by the action, she clutched him to her, muttering, "Fuck, fuck. Cunt. My cunt. Fuck it," in her broken monotone.

Disgusted, Andy started jabbing his cock viciously into her, interspersing his movements with hard pinches on her body. She moaned loudly and then her voice increased its mutterings. Her eyes were closed, her legs splayed. Only her hands, roving over his body, and her mouth muttering its constant stream were moving.

Andy rose over her, cresting like a wave. He shook her hips viciously, and she responded by a fresh flood of words from her mouth and liquid from her cunt. The mingled juices ran down her thighs as Andy's cock spurted into her and ran down the crack of her ass.

He rose to his knees and looked down at her. Her eyes slowly opened.

"I have to get back to my hotel. Where can I find a taxi?" he asked.

She reached for him, then lay back and pinched her nipples. Her eyes were glazed and he could now see that her breasts and belly were covered by blue bruise marks. Judging by what she was doing to herself, they were self-inflicted.

"Some more," she groaned. Her legs spread and her knees in the air. She pulled at him and Andy slapped her hands away. "Yes, yes, do that, but give me some more." Her eyes were closed.

Andy reached for his clothes. "No. I have to go."

"Bring me a Coke, from the fridge," she whispered. The tiny fridge yielded a bottle. He popped the cap, took several sips, then handed it to her.

"Fuck me some more," she said. She spread her legs again in invitation, then stroked the lips with a thumb. "I'm ready for you. Put it in me . . ."

When he did not respond, she dug her thumb into her own dark pink hole, then rubbed it suggestively around the lips. For a moment Andy was tempted to stay, but there was something frenetic about the woman he did not care for, and in any case, he was fucked out and tired. "No," he said shortly and rose to go.

She grinned at him maliciously, then emptied the Coke bottle with one gulp. She held the bottle for a second, then brought it to her cunt. She shoved it in and began masturbating herself. Andy paused to stare. She looked at him for a moment, then he was forgotten as her sensations overcame her. She began to pant, ramming the glass dildo into her cunt as deeply as she could. Her eyes closed and she fell back onto the *futon* Andy had forgotten or ignored. He stepped to the entrance and looked back. The last sight he had of her was the soles of her feet and between them the glass butt of the bottle being pushed rapidly in and out of her gaping cunt.

Jim returned to the lounge to find that the group of young people was still there. On the basis of his acquaintanceship with Nakabe, whom they knew, they made him welcome.

When he put himself out, Jim could be a charming companion. He told jokes, ordered drinks, and generally comported himself as a senior amongst juniors. Town crow talks to village crow, he thought wryly. As subtly as he could, he set himself to charm Mineko. Her eyelashes fluttered up at him, and she seemed to listen with fascination and total concentration to every remark he made.

The entire group staggered down to the street and set off to find taxis to take them home. Through adroit manipulation of seats in the two taxis that arrived, Jim found himself in the rear of a car with Mineko and one of the young men. Too drunk to care about the couple in the back, he was let off near his home.

Jim ordered the taxi on. His arm was around the girl's

shoulders. "Where shall we go?" he asked, his breath caressing her neck.

"My home of course," she whispered back.

"No, it is such a nice night. We should make the best of it." Very gently he kissed her exposed neck. She shivered, but did not draw away from the caress.

He grew bolder, whispering his adoration into her ear while exploring her body gently through her clothes.

"No, no," she protested softly, but unconvincingly.

The taxi stopped.

"We are here," she said with some relief.

"Where?" Jim asked, sunk in a daze of lust.

"The company dormitory where I live."

"I'll come with you," he said after paying off the taxi.

"No, you can't," she protested. "It is not allowed. Besides, I sleep in a room with another girl . . ."

"But I must say good night to you properly, and it is starting to rain . . ."

She looked at him doubtfully from luminous eyes, and then seemed to overcome some internal scruple. "Come," she said, pulling his hand. "There is a side door to the small *Chanoyu* tea ceremony room. I have the key."

They clung to one another on the sweet smelling *tatami* and Jim was reminded of the frightened inexperienced graspings and squirmings of his high school days. In another way, too, it was similar: she would let him touch and stroke her wherever he wanted outside her clothes, but the most she let him touch with his bare hands were her breasts and her blouse.

She held him on the floor, rubbing her hips desperately against his, clasping at his back. He stroked the length of her figure, his cock an unsatisfied bludgeon in his pants. When he tried to lower a hand to his fly, she grasped at the intruder, fearing for the integrity of her own clothes.

"No, Suzuki-san. No, you must not . . ." She was almost crying. Jim kissed her deeply and she responded as ardently as before, grinding her hips mercilessly against his. He felt her full breasts and she urged him on, lowering his lips to her bosom. He bit the nipples gently through the fabric and she pulled his head closer, then fumbled with her waistband and raised the hem of her blouse. He moved back to help her and exposed her breasts.

They were full and the nipples tumescent. In the dark they appeared as black grapes which stimulated him to a frenzy. She moaned, hiding the sound with her arm. His hand reached between her legs and she clamped her thighs and rolled away from him, panting heavily.

"Please, Suzuki-san, please. You must go. . . ." One of her breasts, still exposed in the dark, rose and fell with the power of her breathing. He made a move towards her and she fled to the side, her face a mask of wretchedness. He knew she was on the verge of fleeing altogether.

"Its all right, baby," Jim said in English, then in Japanese, keeping a soothing tone, "You will see me again? When I come back?"

"Of course," she breathed in relief. "Of course I will."

He rose and slipped into the night. She shut the door behind him and Jim bent over with the pain of frustration in his balls. Walking as gently as he could, he headed on foot back to the hotel and bed. The slight drizzle cooled his ardor as he walked through the dark night.

# CHAPTER 4:

# LOVE OF THE GODS

Towards nightfall they alighted from the small bus that had brought them from Gifu. The memories of the previous night were still on them. The mountains, glowing purple with the sunset and dark blue with the shadows hid secrets they only hinted at. Andy took a deep breath, filling his lungs with the clear mountain air. "Just look at that," he said admiringly.

The lower parts of the mountains, leading up from the stream at their feet were terraced, sculpted by the hand of man. Higher up they yielded to regular outlines of cultivated forests. Through some of the trees they could see the outlines of farmhouses and small clusters of hamlets. Television antennae flashed in the ending light and they could hear, from somewhere behind them in the small village, the sounds of children playing baseball.

"You know what I'd like?" said Jim thoughtfully "I'd like to sleep outside for once."

"Where?" asked Andy pragmatically.

Jim shrugged. "We'll find a place."

They bought some supplies from a small grocery: *miso shiru* soup powder, crackers and processed cheese, a salami ("Probably made of whale meat considering how little it cost," Andy commented, making a face), and a can of jellylike *an-mitsu* for dessert.

They rambled down the road, ignoring the curious looks of passers by. A kilometer out of the village they spotted a small uninhabited temple. Without discussion, they headed for it. The broad ramshackle roof sheltered a wide wooden veranda, the wood dusty and unused. The garden had been abandoned and stray bushes grew everywhere amidst the rank grasses. A small stone *stupa,* the characters on its meter-high sides worn through, lay canted to one side.

They carefully lit a fire and cooked their supper away from the tinder-dry structure, then, as the clouds came out, crept into their sleeping bags.

"Real traditional," Jim heard Andy say sleepily just as he drifted off to sleep. "Two pilgrims sleeping in an abandoned temple."

They drifted off to the sound of the frogs and the unheard sound of mist.

Something was tickling his nose. Andy woke with a shiver, and immediately sneezed hugely. He saw stars which giggled delightfully. For a moment he accepted the sound without question. Then his mental processes went into gear with a jerk and he opened his eyes wider. A figure was crouched by his head, and the giggles were evidence of the figure's female nature. He saw something long come at his face again and he twisted his head away. The grass stem jiggled before his nose to the renewed sound of giggling.

"Afraid of my sword, O traveller?" the female's voice was mocking him. He rose to sit in the sack, grinning.

"Can I help you, miss?" he said formally.

"Oh, so the peasant can be polite," she answered using the same archaic politeness he had used. He laughed with her this time. He could not compete with her in trading insults based on levels of politeness.

"Who are you?" he asked.

In the darkness she shifted and said with a smile in her voice "What do you care?"

Andy peered at her again. She was barefoot and wore a light—too light for the weather—*yukata* robe. As she was squatting right before his face it was perfectly obvious that she wore nothing else underneath. Even in the dark her flesh glimmered and the black patch of her pussy was perfectly obvious.

"Aren't you cold?" he asked. The question was only partly disinterested and she sensed it.

"What do you care?" she asked again, her chin jutting forward.

"I wouldn't want you to get sick. . . ." He grinned at her through the dark.

"A gentleman would know what to do then," this time there was a pout in her voice, the sort of tone that reminded him of the spoiled high school girls wheedling their mamas in the Harajuku shopping area, and, more immediately, of Natsumi, a girl who had been partly responsible for uncovering the secret of the Clouds and Rain Company. The memory of Natsumi raised a warmth in his groin. Slowly so as not to startle or scare the village girl he zipped down the side of the sleeping bag and raised the flap while reaching for her knee with the other hand.

She laughed throatily and for one moment sounded not like the village girl she had earlier seemed, but like a mature woman. She slipped easily into the sleeping bag, resting her head upon his chest.

He stroked her shoulders lightly for a moment, then grew bolder and reached for the soft breast crushed between their bodies.

"It's too hot here," she whined complainingly. With one hand she flipped the sleeping bag completely open, with the other she reached for her robe. It slipped off her shoulders revealing milky white skin highlighted by the dark pinpoints of her nipples and the darker area at the junction of her thighs. She pushed him onto his back then straddled the supine male body.

Andy felt the warmth of her thighs encircling his own, then was lost to the sensation of her silky hand expertly grasping his semierect penis. He looked down and could see only the head jutting from her fist. She raised herself slightly and brought the tip of his flesh to the fur of her opening. With slight delicate motions she rubbed against her crotch. The tip found the upper border of her opening and she held it there, pushed against her femaleness while the male monster grew in her fist. Bending his cock still further backwards she introduced the inflamed tip between the soft inner lips of her demanding hole.

Andy gasped and almost rose to a sitting position. Her cunt seemed equipped with muscles of its own. He felt his rampant cock being sucked in, almost against his will, into a demanding maelstrom of snaky muscular slithery movement. She settled on him, her hips light as a feather, her lower mouth sucking at him with smooth undeniable muscular contractions.

Andy arced his hips high, wanting to stab her to the quick, to return some of the cutting pleasure she was giving him. She smiled down at him through the strands of hair that were straying out of the bunch tied at her nape. He reached for her small breasts, teasing and pinching them. At first his fingers were gentle, but she urged him

on, first by voice, then merely by rewarding him with
extra powerful sucks of her vagina as his fingers squeezed
her dark nipples.

He closed his eyes the better to satisfy and sharpen his
sense of touch. Her hot channel was flooded with slick
smooth liquid, and yet each thrust of his loins, each
descent of hers onto his impaling shaft was a smoothly
balanced struggle that brought him ever closer to massive
orgasm.

Andy dug his heels into the hard wooden floor, inadequately masked by the fabric and lining of the bag when
she smoothly rose off him. He clutched at her, and through
her legs he could see a similar female figure crouched over
Jim. Before he could absorb what was happening she had
turned lithely and was crouching over his head. The warm
damp musk covered his nose and as his tongue licked out
he found that his oral digit too was sucked into her
demanding channel. It was like kissing a particularly skillful, beautifully tasting mouth, he thought in a moment of
sanity. The warm cavern of her mouth had descended on
his shaft and engulfed it. Sharp little teeth were teasing
the bottom side of the erect maleness, and her lips and
tongue sucked demandingly at him. Thought was impossible as waves of pleasure caused his frame to tremble and
jerk. His balls contracted spasmodically. For the first time
in his life Andy felt the actual progress of his sperm
through the channel of his cock. His tongue and cock
both held prisoner, both struggling to imprison themselves
deeper, he spurted semen into her welcoming mouth, his
hips arcing wildly off the floor.

He collapsed back onto the floor breathing heavily. The
girl disappeared for a moment, whisking around until her
face hovered over his. She kissed his lips lightly, and her
mouth tasted faintly salty from the residue of his sperm.

He held her weakly to his chest as she began fluttering kisses over his cheeks, nose, and lips. Gradually the kisses became longer, slower, more demanding. Her tongue flicked out to lave his ear, then her teeth were at his neck and shoulders, biting gently, ever demanding.

To his surprise Andy found himself responding. His cock which had seemed completely drained only a moment before rose to its stiff glory. Currents seemed to flow from her lips through his skin to center in the pit of his belly. He stroked her rounded body, the wide hips and smooth skin begging his attention. He felt the crack between the mounds of her ass. Her moisture was still flowing copiously and he wetted her buns with her own juices. Urging him on she rubbed the full length of her smooth soft flesh against his frame.

Andy rolled her onto her back and mounted himself between her thighs. His cock it seemed needed no guidance. Almost before he was ready for it he found himself being sucked into her narrow vagina, urged on by the clutch of her heels against his rump. Andy found that he had no need to move. The village girl was stronger than she appeared. She supported his larger frame easily, and her cunt worked for both of them, sucking him deeper into her demanding furnace. He squirmed over her, rubbing his hairy pubis as strongly as he could into her soft mound. She responded by breathing into his ear a low moaning sound that brought him, jerking and snorting, to a renewed climax. The second time was as intense as the first. His cock squeezed and spat its milky offering at the willing demanding door of her cervix. Her tiny heels drummed into his back and her hands stroked his shoulders with a firmness that made him long for more. He came, then came again, and when he thought he would not be good for anything else, she milked him one more time, then curled up next to his back for some rest. Later still he awoke to find his cock encased in a cool mouth that sucked and forced it to rise to all its glory. How she did it he never did manage to figure out, but with a lithe squirming she had changed direction and was soon riding him to further climaxes.

Far off in the distance, Andy heard the sound of a cock crowing. He rolled to the side, his cock still painfully erect. The girl rose without a word, draped her *yukata* casually over her shoulders and stepped over to where Jim was lying. Blearily Andy could make out another female figure crouched over Jim's thighs. For a moment there was something almost predatory about the hunched figure. Then Andy's lover shook the other girl's shoulder and said something in a murmur too light for him to hear. The other girl rose, too, and without a word redonned and retied her robe. In the growing sudden pre-dawn darkness they stepped off the wooden temple platform and were gone.

"How was it?" Andy managed to croak across the distance to his brother. He was answered only by an exhausted snore as he too dropped off to sleep.

The two of them hoisted their packs with difficulty. Both had deep dark rings under their eyes. The cool morning air invigorated them and they marched out of the temple onto the narrow mountain road. The sound of a tiny two-wheel tractor hauling a car came from behind them. The farmer peered down at them as he passed. Andy was used to the surprised stares at his direction from villagers. Few had seen non-Japanese in the flesh, all were curious. The tiny motor on wheels put-putted down the road for a short distance, then stopped. The farmer turned in his seat to watch them approach.

"Good morning. Lovely weather, isn't?"

"Good morning. Yes, fine weather," Jim answered.

"You two gentlemen're from the city?"

"Yes."

"Hiking eh? Nice weather for it. Where did you sleep the night?"

Andy took it for the common politeness of the average Japanese towards a stranger. "Back there," he said offhandedly, waving in the general direction of the temple.

"The old temple?" The farmer's grizzled eyebrows rose over his face and he seemed puzzled. "Eh well, few of us care to do so, but you younger folk. . . ."

"It's not so bad, one night in the open, and the roof is good shelter." Jim laughed.

"Ayah, so it is. But we around here believe its haunted you see."

Jim laughed again. Andy was politely hiding his grin. "Didn't see any ghosts."

"No? Well, just goes to show y'can't believe everything you hear. Used to be inhabited by two young women fleeing the Restoration wars in the nineteenth century. Both died, or disappeared anyway. Former concubines of some provincial lord I've heard." He turned to the handlebars of his tractor and the little machine started put-putting furiously again. The elderly farmer drove off and the two young men stared at his retreating back in silence.

"Pulling our leg, wasn't he?" one of them said as they took up the march again.

# CHAPTER 5:

# LOVE OF THE MOUNTAINS

"How about walking today?" Andy suggested. He had been looking at the road map.

Jim looked at him doubtfully. "Where to?"

"Instead of going down to this intersection then angling north, why not cut across this pass here . . . Then we can just walk north . . ."

Jim studied the map. Half-forgotten map reading skills struggled to return. "OK," he said finally. Doubt overlaid his words. They found a path leading in the direction they hoped to go and set off.

They climbed slowly up and through the mountain range. On the map the path looked easy, but as the day wore on Andy decided the map was a liar. They climbed through forests of pine and cedar, pacing occasionally along tiny rice paddies. Sometimes a paved road went their way for a while, and they followed with alacrity, then turned off into the depths of a forested hill.

By the afternoon they were stopping every half hour.

"The guide says there ought to be a *minshuku* around here somewhere," Jim said, peering at the map as if hoping to find the inn among its pages.

"You've been saying that for the past two hours," Andy groaned. He hobbled on grimly, hoping only for a bath and a cold beer.

A two-storied wooden building peeped at them from among the trees. They struggled up to it and found a narrow paved road leading off into the forest which they followed to the front door. "Asahikawa Minshuku" a sign beside the dilapidated gate announced. The two young men looked at one another. Salvation at last. A cheap inn was just what the doctor ordered. Urgently.

"*Gomen kudasai,*" they called out politely at the door.

"Come in please, come in please," a plump short-haired elderly woman bowed them in. "Would you be wanting a room?"

They nodded, too tired to talk, and were ushered into a dark hall and through an elderly corridor whose polished wood groaned as they walked over it. They deposited their packs in the small tatami room. In actuality it was only a section of a larger hall that had once served as the central hall of the farmhouse the inn had previously been. Rooms were created by adding or subtracting heavy wooden *fusuma* or lighter paper glazed *shoji* doors.

Andy's muscles were knotted from the day's climb. Jim was talking to the elderly innkeeper, and he decided to take a bath. He wandered through the small old wooden structure of the inn until he found the bath. The tub was small for an inn, but the water was clear indicating Andy was the first bather. Clear light, the last of the day came in through a white translucent pane.

He stripped rapidly and dipped one of the small plastic

buckets lining the wall into the water, then thoughtlessly splashed it over himself. He leaped up, cursing. The water came close to boiling his skin. He tried again, more cautiously this time, sloshing water carefully over his body while squatting next to the sunken bath. The room gradually filled with steam and he lathered himself luxuriously.

The door slid open just as he found himself contorted into an impossible position, trying to scrub his back. The young female figure backed into the bathroom and closed the sliding door to the dressing room. They both recoiled, Andy skipping on the wet soapy floor and banging his elbow painfully. The girl, seen hazily through the steam, covered her mouth with one hand and tried unsuccessfully to hide the juncture of her legs with the other while twisting away to hide her breasts. She slipped too and ended up in a pile on the floor.

Andy groaned as he tried to straighten up.

"Are you hurt?" she cried in alarm, her modesty overcome by the damage she thought she had caused. "I am so terribly sorry . . ."

"Nothing to be sorry about, not your fault," Andy groaned. "I was trying to scrub my back . . ." He tried to demonstrate and groaned again. His muscles had pulled into a knot. He turned away from her for modesty's sake and was surprised to find that she had not retreated.

"What country are you from?"

"Finland," said Andy perversely.

Her eyes widened. "I have never met anyone from Finland. Where is that, please?"

He laughed and resumed his scrubbing.

"May I please?" she asked timidly, reaching for his scrubbing cloth.

"Why, thank you," Andy replied, his interest perking. "Are you hiking, too?"

"Yes. Going through the mountain on foot. The Kiso range is so beautiful this season." She scrubbed brusquely at his back.

Inevitably, particularly as portions of her anatomy came into contact with his back, his thoughts turned elsewhere. He hoped she would do her work thoroughly, as a pillar of flesh grew between his thighs. She leaned over him, staring down at his shoulder, between his legs, and for one moment he felt the pressure of her soft breasts and belly against his back. His cock sprung erect and he turned to reach for her just as she withdrew. There were sounds of female voices from the dressing-room. A splash of water hit his shoulders and Andy automatically said, "Thank you."

"You had better get in and soak," she said pragmatically, rising to her feet. "Other club members are coming. I will warn them the bath is in use." There was an unfathomable look on her face as she walked unselfconsciously to the door and let herself out.

"It's occupied," he heard her say as the door closed and he slipped into the warm waters.

"If those bints hadn't turned up just then, I'd have been in her," Andy said bitterly to Jim over supper. At the next table the mountaineering club—all nine of them—chattered over their meal of rice, soup, and grilled fish.

"They seem impressed by you," Jim grunted. His muscles ached from the strain of walking.

"I wonder if I could get one of them alone for a while . . . ?"

"Not easy, you know how these clubs are," Jim countered.

The girls started singing, and one, encouraged by the others, approached the two. "Would you like to join us?" she asked shyly.

Jim smiled broadly, all pains forgotten. "Of course we will." Andy groaned, but joined the fun nonetheless. They introduced themselves and were introduced to the climbing team in turn. They were students, starting a new year as is the custom with a training camp. Andy enjoyed watching them. They were as bouncy and jolly as puppies out on a romp. Bronzed faces betrayed the fact that they had been out for several days, and there was much good natured laughter and in-jokes in which he and Jim had no share. But every once in a while a calculating look came his way from one or another of the girls. He caught one of the glances and winked, but the girl, slim and short, ignored the overture and looked away, her face blank. He wished he knew what they were thinking.

Later, ensconced in the thick bedding that Japanese inns provide, he grew hard as he speculated on the self-protected woman flesh on the other side of the *fusuma*.

"How is it that a guy can be dead tired, yet have a prong as hard as iron?" Jim wondered aloud in the dark.

Andy merely chuckled as he turned over on his side.

There was much giggling on the other side of the *fusuma* door. Andy groaned silently. If that went on, the pyjama-party like atmosphere was going to cost him a night's sleep. A particularly loud burst of giggles ended with whispers. In the glow of the night light Andy could see that Jim too was awake.

"Gonna drive me crazy," Andy muttered.

"Yeah," Jim whispered back. "But it's not the noise. My dong is still as hard as the Monkey King's club and I can't see any solution except my hand." He jerked his shaft roughly and his quilt jumped. There was another burst of whispers and then some more loud giggles.

The *fusuma* between the two rooms slid open. "Jimu-

san, Andzy-san, are you awake? Are we bothering you?''
Two female faces peered into the room shyly.

"Actually, we weren't ready to sleep," Andy protested
untruthfully. "Just talking."

"Then would you like to join us?" asked one of the
faces in the gloom.

"Of course," Andy said with alacrity. He slipped out
of the covers and slid over the old *tatami* mats into the
other room. The quilts in the small room were touching
one another, forming a single expanse of bedding. The
girls had been lying, heads towards the center of the room,
and nine pairs of eyes examined him as he sat on the
bedding, shivering a little. The mountain air was cold,
notwithstanding the closed windows and shutters.

"It's cold," he complained.

"Please, cover yourself," one of the girls invited raising a corner of her quilt.

Not knowing if the invitation was meant as he preferred
to hear it, Andy hastily slipped under the closest quilt. He
was greeted by some more giggles, and asked about their
plans for the morrow. They talked of their itinerary, and
a voice out of the gloom asked if he and "Jimu-san"
would like to come along.

"Too much for an old man like me," he replied and
was answered with a burst of laughter.

"I don't think you are old," the girl whose quilt he
was sharing said in a whisper. Her hand crept along his
arm as if in consolation.

"No! He's cute!" an anonymous voice said in the
gloom to the accompaniment of giggles of approval.

Jim appeared, and Andy realized that the delay was
caused by need to beat his rampant erection into submis-
sion. Even so, there was a noticeable bulge in the darker
man's *yukata*. Jim saw the situation without Andy having

to say a word, and slid himself under the nearest thick quilt in the other row.

"Who's got a story?" they choroused. "A ghost story!"

"It's not midsummer yet!" another female voice complained.

"Yes, but we're up in the mountains!"

"I'll tell a story," Andy volunteered. "A *gaijin* ghost story. But I must not be disturbed . . ." he began a tale, greatly embellished by his own imagination of the legend of Sleepy Hollow. His audience shrieked appreciatively at each turn and twist, and the girl in whose *futon* he was sheltering trembled and nestled into his body. Not unnaturally, he began to react. Her arm touched the man gristle, and without betraying her interest in any muscle of her face, she began exploring the new phenomenon. From that point on Andy's recitation grew more ragged.

First she stroked the length through the fabric of the *yukata* he wore. He obliged by poking himself forward. Her innocent eyes peering at his face she exposed the length of the shaft and stroked the silky tip. The feeling emboldened her for her small hands encircled the manroot, then rubbed the glans unhurriedly. She touched the tiny hole, already running with its tiny transparent teardrop. Feeling for the bag beneath she squeezed it too hard and Andy turned his scream in time to a replica of a goblin's cry.

Finally the young woman turned away from him. She bent carefully at the waist, exposing her buttocks and the full lips of her cunt to his attack. Easily and without hurry she guided him to her pussy lips. Andy kept on talking though he was near the end of his control. His words came out jumbled as he hurried to finish his tale. As the headless horseman charged forward, she pushed herself into his erection. He felt the resistance and narrowness of her cunt and realized that she was a virgin. Anxious to aid her, and to relieve himself, he finished his story with a flourish of his hands and a shout. The girls shrieked in their bedding in delicious fright just as his partner pushed her ass backwards and he shoved forward. Her scream was not of surprise, but of delight at the pain of losing her maidenhead. From that point on Andy's way became easier. She nestled back into his arms as someone else started a story in the dark, and he shafted her lightly, careful to make no betraying move outside the cover. She cried out once again as the climax to the second story arrived in opportune time to camouflage her own. Almost before she was finished Andy felt another pair of hands reaching for him. He pulled out of her ravaged cunt and allowed himself to be led, creeping, to the next *futon* in line.

Jim found himself lying close to a plump muscular figure. Her bare calf and clothed form touched his skin at every possible point. He felt her shiver as the story progressed. His cock grew hard, poking at her side. She nestled closer, perhaps not knowing the meaning of the hard object. His hand drifted to her haunch, and when there was no response, he stroked her side, lingering over the touch of her ass.

She turned to face him in the dark. "I have never had a man," she whispered into his ear. Her breath and a strand of her long hair brushed his ear. "I want you. No one will know. . . ."

Jim felt between her legs. She was moist and ready, her full plump thighs parted for his inspection. In the dark he mounted between her legs, kissing her exposed breasts as he did so, then searching for her mouth with his tongue. She touched his skin lightly, feeling for his ass, daring to fondle his hairy bag as he prepared to enter her.

Jim slid into the plump girl, hiding his groan of relief.

The tension in the close air of the room was palpable. None of the other girls looked in their direction. The plump girl shrieked lightly as he entered but her shriek was just a counterpoint to the nervous giggles that accompanied the ghost story. Jim stroked her body gently without moving. She had full breasts, now uncovered below his palms. She clung to him, one thigh over his. Without pushing too rapidly he gradually widened the opening for his cock. She breathed harshly into his ear, the sounds masked by her friends.

The next girl in line, Andy found, was much more aggressive than her friend had been. Perhaps it was the consciousness that she was not the first, or the feel of the two bodies beside her, perhaps the bottle of cheap sake whose smell permeated the air had gone the rounds again. In any case, she was both eager and willing, and the muffled shriek of joy as he entered her was clear above the storyteller's voice. No one noticed, or at least, made any outward signs of noticing, and Andy set to work with a will, throwing all caution to the winds as he shafted her with abandon.

As he rolled off, Andy found himself being pulled under the quilt of the next girl in line. Unlike her predecessor this one was determined to feel the entire weight of the male as she was entered for the first time. She grasped his prick expectantly and inexpertly and her lips parted at the strange feel and size. Nonetheless she guided the tip of the manroot to her waiting canal. Her hips rose to meet his. Nothing loathe, Andy surged forward and pressed against her moist ready opening. The soft downlike fur parted beneath his charge and he could feel the gradual widening of the channel as it readied itself for his assault. He tried to concentrate on the sensation at the tip of his prick. He imagined he could feel the delicate membrane

parting before the thrust of his flesh. Andy drew a sharp
breath at the tight feel of her pussy channel, then shafted
her steadily and inexorably. She responded by putting her
mouth to his and forcing him deeply into her. The pain
of penetration she translated into a bite as she fought his
lips and drew blood. Andy withdrew his mouth. He could
taste blood, his own blood, on his lips. She pulled his
head to her again and kissed him fiercely, using her teeth
freely. In self-defense he struck back, jamming his shaft
to the balls into her. He lowered one hand and felt her
virginal blood coating the hairs at the base of his cock.
He wished he could turn on the light and see the damage
he had caused. Her tongue thrust as deeply into him as he
was in her, and her teeth extended their vengeance for the
blood he was shedding below.

Andy started moving slowly in her. His tempo increased
as she sought to reach her first orgasm with a man. She
nuzzled at his neck and shoulders, sought the flavors of
his armpits. Her snuffling was so loud Andy knew the
other girls were listening avidly, though the stream of
anecdotes and ghost stories never ceased. She clutched at
his hard bottom with blunt fingers and her hips cradled
him and rose beneath like a wave. Her blocky muscular
body jerked once, then again. Her eyes closed and her
head fell back. The dark hollow of her mouth, rimmed
whitely with sharp teeth was open in a silent howl. The
tremors of her frame subsided and her hands fell limply
by her side. Andy slipped off and his foot touched another
eagerly waiting calf. Through the dimness a dark pair of
eyes under a page-boy haircut peered at him appealingly.

Sometime later he touched skin that was harder and
hairier than what he had felt before. "Oops, pardon my
dear Gaston. Are you quite finished here?"

Jim chuckled. "After you, my dear Alphonse. Did you

leave anything for me?'' He slid over his brother and resumed where Andy had left off. Andy reached for the girl Jim had been fucking and continued on his self-appointed and publicly-supported rounds.

She was a fine plump girl with long hair and she reached for Jim avidly. It was clear that her recent introduction to male love had not been sufficient. Jim had no idea what Andy had taught or shown her, but it was clear she was an avid pupil. She locked full lips into his. He examined her torn cunt with a questing finger. She hissed at the sting, but did not draw back. Instead her hand grabbed at his and forced three of his fingers deep inside her.

"Outside first," he chuckled into her ear.

"Inside!" she demanded. "The outside I know myself." Then she began to explore him with a thoroughness and dedication he would have liked to pursue with greater thoroughness. She ran fingers down his spine, then back again, tracing each muscle as she came to it. With her other hand she guided Jim into her cunt. It was overflowing with her juices, mingled with drying sticky blood. The thought that Andy had been in the same place a few minutes before spurred Jim on. Her hand descended to his bobbing ass and she pinched his buns hard. His pace increased. Her fingers dipped between his ass cheeks, then she fingered his asshole while at the same time guiding his lips to her flat broad breasts. He sucked in a nipple, then bit it, and tried to remove her hand from his behind. She brought her finger to her mouth, unperturbed, moistened the digit then returned it to explore his bottom more gently.

Her interest was aroused by his wrinkled ball bag. She cuddled it as gently as she could, then explored the join of their bodies. Her other hand guided him alternatively

from breast to breast, and he sucked at the erect nubbin
faithfully.

"You are wonderful," she muttered. "Wonderful . .
wonderful . . . wonderful . . ." she began repeating in a
dazed litany. The speed of his thrusts increased. Her body
tensed and her explorations, which had been controlled
and cool at first, deteriorated to a frenzied clutching a
handfuls of his skin and frame. She breathed harshly with
each thrust and repeated her refrain of wonderful. The
whites of her eyes rolled back and she started to scream
her frame locked as rigidly as a tetanus patient's. Jim
hastily clamped his mouth over hers and licked her unre
sponsive tongue. Gradually the rigidity of her frame
passed. Her eyes returned to normal and she stared through
the gloom at him.

"That was better than I ever hoped for," she whispered
"Fat girls don't have much choice, but this has been
super. My name is Baba Matsuko. Remember it. I will
remember you. Both of you." She stared at him discon
certingly just as a slim hand inserted into the *futon* found
Jim's erection and dragged him over to the next demand
ing woman.

"Well, that's the last one, girls," it was the club presi
dent's authoritative voice that spoke in the dimness. She
reached up her hand and switched off the light. "We must
get our sleep. And our noise must not disturb our two
neighbors."

The hint was well taken. Jim roused himself. He shook
Andy who had fallen into a doze, his face streaky with
sweat. The two of them quietly slid the *fusuma* open and
crawled back to their own room.

"Quite cool for a girl who's just lost her virginity and
been fucked twice . . ."

"Were all of yours. . . ."

"Only the first five bro. Then I reached your handi-
work . . ."

"*I* had five virgins . . ."

"What the hell, four, five, what's the difference? More
than I thought existed in the whole wide world."

The sun, tracing a path across the golden tatami roused
them from their exhausted sleep. Rubbing his tousled hair
Andy slid open the door to the other room. The *futon* had
been neatly stacked, the room was empty. There was no
sign of anything that had taken place the night before.
Even the lingering smells of love had been absorbed by
that prefect air cleaner, the *tatami*. Under a *futon* he spied
a trace of white. One of the girls had forgotten a sleeping
robe. Its blue and white pattern was marred in the center
by a tiny drop of brownish red. He smiled and touched it
gently with his forefinger.

# CHAPTER 6:

# CYCLING AWAY

They reached the fork in the path the innkeeper had told them about by noon. The trail was clearly marked. Not far below them a major highway snaked through the mountains. They walked along the path which brought them, in small gradations, higher up the mountain and into the pass proper. Above them, on another mountain, they could barely make out several colorful moving dots. Jim pointed them out to Andy who grinned.

"Mountain climbers indeed," he said.

"No one would believe us," Jim said, returning the grin.

"Believe that they are a mountain climbing club?"

"No, you fool. That we had nine virgins in one night."

Andy laughed. "Only half that," he said in mock modesty.

The hiking path now moved away from the highway which sped through a tunnel. The air was quieter now and they reached a more gradual slope where they stopped to catch their breaths. Around them rose a forest of pine and other evergreens. They stepped into a large clearing created by the loggers who tended the forest, then found a comfortable shaded area under a spreading bush. The shade and the grass-like growths they were reposing on crept insidiously into their senses. Before they knew it, both were asleep, having barely touched their lunch of pickled-plum centered rice balls.

Jim's head was hammering as he woke from his sleep. At first he thought it the result of sleeping at midday, then he realized the racket was coming from outside. From all around them in fact. Andy woke too and started to jump to his feet when Jim managed to identify the source of the racket. He grabbed his brother and pulled him down to shelter amongst the bushes' branches.

"Stay down you fool!" he said tensely.

"What's the matter?" asked Andy, still befuddled from the rude awakening.

Jim carefully moved some branches to create a peephole. "Look," he said. "*Bosozoku.*"

The motorcycle gang was circling the clearing, driving their bikes wildly in complicated patterns. The dust and smoke from their exhausts added to the confusion. Only gradually did the picture begin making sense.

"A rumble, huh!?" Andy said casually.

"Yeah, and if they see us here, we'll be in it, too. Get down, dammit."

Andy casually obeyed and they peeked cautiously at the scene before them.

The bikers had finally resolved themselves into two groups. On the twins' left was a group led by a bareheaded youth in black leather wearing dark bike goggles. The rest of his crew were also dressed mainly in black. There was a smattering of pillion riders on some of the bikes. All the back-seat riders were female, mostly wearing black leather jackets or other black items of dress. A few wore full black jumpsuits.

The other side was arrayed mainly in red. All the bikes sported red banners flying from the rear of their saddles, and both men and girls sported red scarves. The two lines yelled and taunted one another, flourishing knives, chains, and a multitude of iron bars. Occasionally a biker from one side or another would gun his bike and feint towards the line of the other group, only to wheel back as soon as the opposition mounted.

"Go away, shoo," said Andy under his breath.

"What's the matter?" Jim asked at this display of belligerence.

"Dying for a pee," muttered the other. It appeared that the stalemate was about to hold for a long while.

Suddenly they heard a rising roar of engines. They came from behind the Black's lines. Three bikes, their red flags flaunted wildly, hurtled through the undergrowth. They cut through the Black line from behind. There was a dusty swirl of action. The noise of screams and bike engines rose to a crescendo. Bikers darted across the clearing, retreated, zoomed in again.

The semiquiet of before was restored as both sides retreated to lick their wounds. Two bikers lay ominously on the ground, groaning feebly, their machines twisted beside them.

The black-clad leader rose on his bike. "Hey, Reds! Reds!" The noise abated somewhat. "You stupid fellows. Look what this attack cost you, hey? Two of your men on the ground. And you lost something else, too!"

Two of the the Blacks, dismounted, advanced. Between them they held the struggling figure of a slim girl. Her hair was a bright red, and a torn red scarf rested around her neck.

"Yeah? Well you can keep her," the head of the Reds answered in a loud voice. "You're careless yourselves, horseheads. And it's your own girl, too, stupid." A Red bike inched forward. On it, her arms held by a muscular biker, rode a girl in black, her helmet still on her head.

"I'll fuck your stupid cow," the Black leader said. "She'll enjoy it more than she enjoys it with you!!"

The girl screamed with a high pitched sound that grated on the nerves. It was obviously a scream of anger, not anguish, and she tried to bite the men holding her. They cuffed her quickly, and she resumed her screaming, mixing the sounds with barely comprehensible imprecations and unflattering descriptions of the Blacks.

Suiting action to words the Black leader motioned to his two men. The two gang members tripped the girl and held the redhead's shoulders on the ground. Another two spread her legs after pulling off her dirty jeans. She was not a natural redhead. She kept on screaming her high pitched scream, like a steam engine gone berserk. The two lines of skirmishers edged towards one another, their engines growling.

Red-scarf yelled something incomprehensible, and the line of his red-flagged cohorts relaxed. The helmeted girl was hauled before him and he raised her to a seat on the gas tank of his bike. Two of his men and one woman helped spread her around him. He reached for the zipper of her leather suit, fumbled with it, cursed, and produced a blade with which he cut at her crotch. She spat curses at him which he ignored. His erect prick sprang into sight and he shouted at his henchmen so that they cleared an alley, making his actions fully visible to the black-clads.

The Black leader slipped back his goggles and called out something as well, then his prick came into view and he shook it in the direction of the enemy leader. When the mere sight had no effect, he knelt quickly between the redhead's thighs and thrust roughly forward. The volume of her screams and curses doubled as he rode rapidly into her.

The red-flag leader thrust forward with his hips as well. The girl said nothing, merely turning her face away from the man's grin. He was quick about it, fucking her roughly and squeezing her form against the frame of his bike. He paused and his jeans-clad ass poised over her for a moment, then jerked spasmodically. He yelled in triumph and hauled her erect on his bike, showing off his prowess to the enemy leader. The girl hung loosely in his hands, her torn outfit dangling about her. When the display had no effect on the Blacks except to increase the volume of their taunts and screams, the Red leader called something to one of his lieutenants. The girl was hustled roughly from the front of his bike to another, and mounted again by a gleeful red-bandana biker whose face was covered with pimples. Throughout the exchange, and the following partners, the black-clad girl said not a word. Nor did any sound come out of her when the female members of the Red gang twisted her nipples cruelly or helped their men rape her by exposing her cunt to their view, hands, and cocks.

The red-headed prisoner of the Blacks was far from silent. She yelled and cursed, more from anger than fear or humiliation. The Black leader rose from her and remounted his bike, and was replaced by other members of the band. Jim could see a muddy pool accumulate beneath her spread legs, and he wondered how she could keep up the flood of threats and curses in her situation. Finally all the men finished. The girl in black was allowed to drop from the last bike, and she lay on the ground, stunned or too tired to move. Redhead ceased cursing as the last of the Blacks left her and remounted his own bike. It seemed as if, with their lust slaked, both bands were at a loss for what to do next. The gunning of motors, the mutual imprecations, even the brandishing of weapons died down.

In the growing quiet a new sound intruded itself: the sound of sirens. The clearing was suddenly full of the sound of two-stroke engines again. The gangs sped out of the clearing in trails of mud. They rode as animals flee before a fire: enemy ignoring enemy in the race away from disaster. Two bodies remained in the clearing, ignored or forgotten by their erstwhile companions.

The two girls seemed completely dazed. Redhead rose and shook her head as if confused at the sounds of the sirens. She hurriedly groped for her jeans. Black-clad rose painfully and tried to tug the shreds of her jump-suit around her. When that did not work she cast a hurried glance around her then ran away from the sound of the approaching sirens.

Jim tugged at Andy. "Come on, let's get the hell out of here. We don't need trouble with either the police or the gangs. Come *on!*"

Andy followed him reluctantly, casting bewildered eyes back at the clearing. Jim headed up the mountain.

"The road's the other way," Andy insisted.

"Yeah, but so are the police and the gangs. Let's get out of here."

They ran rapidly up the mountain their packs jouncing at their backs. Tiring after a hundred meters, their pace slackened. There was the sound of crashing behind them as if someone in rapid pursuit was rushing towards them. Andy stopped and turned down the path.

"What the hell are you doing?" Jim whispered.

"Going towards them. We don't know anything, right? Just came down the path . . ."

Jim mentally debated the point but followed the other. There was a sudden crashing through the bushes besides them and a figure ran into Jim, caromed off him, and tripped Andy just as another figure slammed into him from below. They went down in a tangle of bodies, flailing limbs, and packs. Jim who had been on top when they fell was the first one to pick himself up. He looked down at their assailants in wonder. It was Redhead and Black-leather. Redhead still did not have her pants on and she was breathing wildly, trying to climb to her feet. Andy was sprawled over Black-leather who was sobbing bitterly and trying to fend him off.

They rose and sorted themselves out. Redhead, eyeing the two strangers with disdain, slowly put on her breeches. Andy stared at Black-leather. Her hand went to her crotch. The leather was cut in a wide rip and her black bush was matted with white gluey liquid slatherings. She bit her lip and backed away, the black bug eyes of her helmet staring back at him unfathomably.

Below them they could hear an engine laboring as a large vehicle started moving up the track they were standing on. The two girls stared wildly about.

"Wait," Andy said, moved by an impulse. He felt shamed at what had passed on the girls, and Black-leather's sudden fear left him with an uncomfortable feeling. "Say that you're with us. We'll just walk down . . ."

Redhead nodded and finished zipping up her pants. Black-leather shook her head "I can't. Look at me!"

Jim slipped his pack to the ground and opened it while saying over his shoulder, "Get out of that."

For one moment Black-leather hesitated, modesty or suspicion, Andy was hard put to tell. Then she dropped her helmet and slipped quickly out of her ripped leather jump-suit. Underneath she wore torn and beslimed cheap cotton briefs and a rather soiled bra from which her bruised breasts had been pulled. She stripped and Andy could not forebear a look at her nakedness, then she was rapidly climbing into the jeans and T-shirt Jim threw at her. She pulled her black biker's boots back on and hid their tops under the long jeans. Andy kicked her soiled clothes under a bush, hiding them the best he could. They started down the trail again just as a small black and white police car hove into view.

The two policemen looked at the four hikers with some suspicion. The two Japanese girls peered solemnly back, but the young men, one Japanese, the other a foreigner smiled at them and waved.

"Have you seen any bikers come this way?" one of the policemen asked the young Japanese-looking man.

"No . . ." Jim shook his head. "Though we did hear a lot of bikes a few minutes earlier, from down there," he pointed down the hill.

"I'd suggest you don't go there right now," the policeman said kindly. "There are some bad characters about, and we wouldn't want your foreign friend to feel uncomfortable . . ."

Jim nodded, turned to Andy and said in English, "He says there's some trouble ahead and suggests we go back up the mountain . . ."

"All the way back up? But . . . Oh well, OK. We can take another path." Jim played his part as well as he could, even smiling and saying *"Domo arigato"* in as atrocious an accent as he could muster. Satisfied, the policemen continued on.

The four turned up the mountain, and waved as the

police car, having found a clearing to turn around in, headed back the way it had come.

"What's your name?" Jim asked as they watched the patrol-car's rear light disappear down the path.

"Naoko," said Redhead briefly, concentrating on her walking. She shook the lanky red hair from her face and peered up at Jim.

"Hayashi Emiko" said Black-leather.

"I'm sorry. We watched what happened to you down there," Andy made a vague motion downhill. "There was nothing we could do. There were too many of them."

"It happens," Naoko shrugged and tossed some more hair out of her eyes.

"It is good you did not intervene," Emiko said severely. "The Black Dragons would have torn you limb from limb. They are extremely fierce."

Naoko gave a derisive snort. "If there were any left after the Reds had gotten through with them."

Emiko turned to the redhead, her face blazing. "You . . ." Her hands were raised into claws. The two men stepped between them. "Now now, girls, haven't you had enough? Besides, the cops are still there. . . ." The two subsided, but for the next hour, walked on either sides of the two men who acted as buffers.

It was nearing dark as they reached the head of the pass. On either side they could see lights flitting on as the residents of the valleys below prepared for evening. Far before them a small river of lights indicated the highway's exit from the tunnel.

"We'll have to sleep somewhere out here tonight," said Andy doubtfully. "We'll never get down in the dark." The looming masses of the dark mountains around them, so friendly in daylight, so forbidding now, and the trees leaning slightly in the wind seemed to agree.

"We've only got two sleeping bags, and it's going to be *cold*," Jim commented.

"We could use that," Emiko pointed to a small hut beneath the brow of the mountain.

It proved to be one of the huts erected by the loggers for their use during the season. It was not locked. The interior consisted of a small tree-tatami room. There was a battery operated light, a set of tea cups and kettle, and a small iron stove. But at least it provided shelter from the rising wind.

Outside, hidden by some bushes was a tiny stream emerging from the rocks. They drank their fill and loaded the tea kettle. Andy started a fire and Jim collected wood.

"You have a towel?" Naoko was standing before Andy, the scowl which seemed to be her habitual expression in place.

He handed her a small wash towel silently. Without embarassment she stripped off her jeans and disappeared behind the bushes that hid the stream. Emiko watched her, her own desire for a bath clear on her face, but she said nothing.

"Would you like one, too?" Andy asked.

She nodded silently and he handed her the wash towel from Jim's pack and a bar of soap. "Give some to Naoko, too." She turned and vanished behind the bushes as well. The sound of splashing came through the night air.

Jim finished stacking the deadwood and watched Naoko reappear. She held her washed clothes in her hand and strode naked towards them, apparently unbothered by the cold mountain wind. She was well shaped, though on the slim side. Her red hair, darker at the roots, was washed and hung in stringy locks. She got closer and he noticed the goose bumps on her skin. She settled gracefully by the stove and for the first time gave some sign of feeling, closing her eyes and huddling near the fire. Jim silently handed her a shirt and she thanked him with a glance.

Emiko soon followed. She was shorter than Naoko and her borrowed clothes hung loosely on her. She too hunkered near the stove. She examined her bruised skin silently. "Those bastards," she said, wrinkling her nose.

"Huh!" the redhead retorted. "Yours are hardly better, and stink more."

"The Black Dragons are real warriors!" Emiko snapped. "Your red trash . . . bah, they will suffer for this."

"Now now, girls," both men said soothingly. They were promptly ignored and Emiko rose to her feet smoothly and tossed the cup of tea lees in Naoko's face.

"Stop it!" Jim thundered.

"I'll kill the bitch," Naoko screamed charging at the other. The sudden violent attack took the smaller Emiko by surprise. The tiny hut shook as the two bodies crashed to the *tatami* floor and started rolling around in the confined space. Jim and Andy looked at one another for a second and then dived into the fray. Naoko was fairly easily controlled once Andy got a good arm lock on her and twisted her wrist behind her back. Emiko fought on blindly, using claws and teeth freely on all concerned. Jim could find no better solution then sitting on her, his legs wrapped around her frame and arms, his hands forcing her head down onto the old fragrant *tatami*. He looked at a long scratch on his forearm ruefully.

"Gods," Andy said admiringly from his relatively more comfortable position. "She's really something!"

They panted quietly for a moment, the two girls glaring at one another.

"Can we let you go without a fight?" Andy inquired pleasantly. Jim was too mad to say anything.

"Yeah, yeah," Naoko said. Andy loosened her arm a bit. Emiko merely growled.

"Well?" Jim asked, shaking her roughly.

"OK," she said, still glaring.

The two men released them. As soon as Emiko was free, she leaped for Naoko again. The redhead fell back against Andy. The shirt she had borrowed after her bath popped open exposing her taut breasts while white buttons flew in every direction. Jim had been preparing himself for just such an eventuality, but the ferocity of Emiko's attack caught him by surprise. The four of them struggled in the confines of the cabin. The only human sounds were short screams that came from the two boys as an occasional sharp nail or tooth came into contact with their skins. The short fierce fight ended as before, only this time Andy assisted Jim by pinning Emiko's head between his thighs while lying full length on Naoko whose arm was twisted once again behind her back.

Jim glared at the black-haired girl lying beside him. His legs were wrapped about her torso in a scissors hold and one of her hands were held by his at the small of her back. There were tears of rage in her eyes and she was panting heavily.

"You gotta learn to make love, not war," Andy said, punctuating each word with a slap on an available buttock.

"I'd rather kill her," the redhead panted.

"Not now you won't." Jim was panting heavily and his face was flushed with rage. "You're going to kiss and make up."

"Never!" Emiko howled

Jim pushed her head down between Naoko's thighs. "Kiss her!" he commanded. There was a mad glint in his eye Andy had rarely seen before.

"No!"

He slapped her twice, casually but hard. She glared up at him as Andy watched in wonder.

"Get the other one to do it as well," Jim said to Andy. He held Emiko's head down by twisting her hand higher up her back and with Andy's help managed to strip the overlarge jeans off her struggling form. Andy forced the red hair between Emiko's pale thighs and rubbed Naoko's face forcefully into Emiko's crotch.

"If either of you bites," said Jim in a chilling tone, "I will personally pour hot tea over her face and cunt, then throw her out into the cold."

Either the threat or the close proximity and smell of the sex brought cooperation. Emiko who seemed, in the final analysis, to be the more rational of the two gave in first. A tiny pink tongue tip snaked out and licked cautiously at the hole held open for her by Andy. A second later Jim saw a tongue emerge from between Naoko's gaudily dyed hair and start rooting, hesitantly at first, then with greater confidence at the black-haired girl's waiting cunt. He pinched the long labia between his fingers and pulled them wider apart. He peered down with great interest at the scene until the redhead's nuzzling hid the sight from view.

Within a few minutes the men found they could release the two women. Naoko's hands crept up and cupped Emiko's fuller buttocks, pulling the swampy cunt to her face. Her cheeks were visibly moving as she tried to force her tongue deeper into the sweet fresh cavity. Emiko moaned aloud and redoubled her own efforts. Her fingers joined her mouth and she inserted them as deeply as she was able into the redhead's cunt, tickling the little clitoris with her tongue, and sucking the loose lips as well as she could. The two thrashed about again, only this time it was in the throes of their mutual pleasure. Emiko, who ended up beneath the other, pulled Naoko's buttocks to her, exposing the full length of her rear crack. Andy licked his lips at the sight of the tiny anal button, but Jim restrained him. Naoko was humping over Emiko's active mouth. Her back began quivering as a first orgasm overtook her. Sitting bolt upright over Emiko's face, her hair hanging down, she cried out in sudden pleasure, forcing her fingers deep into the black-hair fringed lips between Emiko's legs. She shuddered again and again, then lowered her face to the other girl's crotch and began energetically seeking out the other's pleasure.

Andy stripped himself rapidly, ready to join the two female bodies. Jim held him back once again.

"No. Wait. I gotta watch this."

Both girls were moaning together now, mouth glued to cunt, lips and tongues moving freely. Every once in a while a shudder would overtake one or the other, and the shudders gradually grew in volume. They learned quickly from one another. Emiko sucked in the salty-sour pearl of Naoko's clitoris, and was soon rewarded with the same sensation the redhead was feeling. She traced the shell-like curves of the other's cunt lips, then paused to kiss and lick the soft hollow inside each thigh. For a long wild eternity she felt as if she were making love to herself. Everything she did was echoed in her own loins. Soon she abandoned herself to her utmost fantasies. Her fingers probed the crannies and holes she had never dared explore in her own body, and had never been explored by any other. Each movement was soon echoed by Naoko, who introduced variations of her own.

Finally, her face streaked with Naoko's juices, Emiko withdrew her head. She breathed deeply, then started rubbing the inside of Naoko's crotch with one finger. She bounced in turn on the single digit Naoko was using. She added a second, then a third, then finally her entire hand was sawing at the soft wetness within. She cried out with passion then spun around, swapping her crotch for her head. The smell coming from Naoko's mouth was overpowering. Emiko recognized her own smell in the aroma rising from the pale mouth and redhair that faced her. She clamped her lips eagerly on the redhead's. Their tongues entwined, their bodies rocked together as they masturbated one another towards a climax.

"We are sisters now," Naoko gasped.

"Yes, yes," Emiko gasped, then her lips glued to the redhead's. They started moving together again, rubbing their mounds in thrusting circles against one another. Both closed their eyes as they stroked one another's backs.

The two men slid down beside the women. Andy held his prick firmly in his hand and guided it defiantly forward. Emiko paid him no attention. He parted her thighs but she struggled only when his motions threatened to separate her from her newly acquired "sister." Andy thrust forward into her warmth and moisture, and she ignored him even when his hands clutched roughly at her thin hips, pulling himself deeply into her. He could feel Jim duplicating his motions from the other side. They coordinated their movements and the pressure of the male bodies on the external sides of the heap drove the girls closer to one another. Emiko cast a glance of gratitude over her shoulder. Naoko ignored the male penetration altogether, her hands running over the other girl's warm skin, delicately fluttering over her closed eyes, arousing her nape.

They gradually found the rhythm and the four bodies moved in unison. The strong male loins providing the thrusting power on either side, both women almost oblivious to the men, delicately struggling to extricate the most out of one another. The men's movements gradually grew rougher, and the women panted with joy as their cunts were mashed together, rubbing them roughly to an exquisite climax.

At the peak Jim and Andy clutched female hips and pulled as deeply into them as they could while the two girls, lips and hairy mounds clamped together, were lost in a world of their own. The male cocks spurted their essence into the waiting cunts. At the juncture of four sets of legs rivulets of white sperm ran and dripped to the old *tatami*. Naoko breathed deeply of their combined aromas, her eyes opened and she looked at the sweat and juice bedecked face of her new "sister." As Emiko recovered from the throes of her orgasm, she kissed her cheek lightly.

Emiko opened her eyes. "Again?" she whispered, almost shyly, her hand slipping tentatively to Naoko's breast. Naoko smiled and hugged her, and her lips began tracing a path down the other's neck and back to paradise.

They woke stiff and rather sore on the following morning. The mountain around them was covered with mist which swirled between the pine trees, hiding then uncovering the landscape below them. They found the path and began walking down it. The day warmed up. The flat valley floor was dotted with rice fields. A small river meandered through its center. Almost directly below them was a small town, its pitched roofed houses shining in the late morning sun. The highway ran around the town, disappearing to the south, in the direction of the Gifu City and Nagoya. Across the valley to the northwest a narrower valley debouched into the main one. Perched on the slope of the mountain Andy could make out a low white structure partly obscured by greenery. He peered at it thoughtfully.

"How well do you know this place?" he asked the girls. Emiko shrugged noncommitantly. The Black Dragons were largely from Nagoya and she did not know the place at all.

"I was born near here," Naoko said. "Got paddy mud in my toes."

"Do you know what that thing across the valley is?" he asked, pointing to the tiny white patch.

She peered at it doubtfully. "It used to be a mansion, put up by someone in the Meiji era, about a hundred years ago. I think some large Osaka company bought it, as a country house or something. . . ."

Jim looked sharply at Andy. "Do they grow a lot of flowers here?" he asked Naoko.

She laughed. "Oh yeah. Everyone including my stuffy relatives is going into hothouse flowers. There's been a great demand for them in recent years."

The two men were very thoughtful as they continued their descent.

# CHAPTER 7:

# TURKISH DELIGHT

They stood and waved at the bus while Emiko's face peered down at them. The rain dripped down into their collars as they turned to go. Naoko had left earlier in another direction. She and Emiko had parted reluctantly, their fingers touching long after the last words had been said. They would meet again, and exchanged addresses before parting. After Naoko had left there was little to do but wait for Emiko's bus in the bus station of the tiny mountain town. The descent from the mountain had taken several hours, and all of them were weary of the walk and the drizzle.

"Love is wonderful, particularly new love," Jim said, staring after the departing bus.

"Nature is wonderful, too," said Andy, peering into the overcast. "But a warm bath would be better."

"Philistine. I saw a sign for a *minshuku* just down the road."

Andy nodded happily. A cheap inn was precisely what they needed.

The *minshuku* was plain as befitting a "people's inn." They could eat in the dining room, a cheerless place with formica topped tables. The room, too, was adequate but cheerless and inactivity palled.

"What we could do is try to reach the mansion," Jim suggested doubtfully. They called up the bus depot. Oddly enough, there was no bus service towards that side of the valley, and the clerk at the information office knew nothing about the place. They tried a taxi next, the driver again mistook their directions and started off down the road in the opposite direction from the one they wanted. He got turned around in the small country roads, and eventually sullenly gave up, not before charging them a small fortune for his services. They gave up finally as the afternoon darkened to gloomy evening. The rain dripping down their collars and making them hunch their shoulders uncomfortably.

They walked through the town and as evening deepened, found a small *sushi* shop. The inside was tiny, room for barely seven people. Bellying up to the counter Andy licked his lips in anticipation.

"What shall we do for you?" the large cheerful cook demanded. He placed a broad aspidistra leaf before each of them and a pale pink mound of pickled thinly sliced ginger on each leaf. A tiny dish with two compartments went alongside, one of the compartments filled with a mound of green horseradish paste. "A drink?" he added, peering at Andy doubtfully. *Gaijin* were uncommon in his experience, and he wasn't sure how to treat this one.

"Beer. Tea," they said simultaneously. The counterman smiled broadly in relief. At least this *gaijin* spoke Japanese like a human being should. Large cups, almost mugs of pale green tea were placed before them and the counterman popped the cap of two bottles of Kirin.

"Let's start with some pickled herring . . ."

"Hai!" the counterman called, scooping up a finger of rice and beginning the work. Within seconds they each had a two pale mouthfuls of flavored rice lying before them. Each small patty was topped by a thin slice of silvery lightly pickled herring.

"Ah," said Andy as the horseradish rose to his nose. "Just like my mother used to make . . ."

"Come on," Jim said. "Our mother probably never even knew there was a thing such as sushi."

"Fat lot you know. Old Mama Middler still makes a mean plate of pickled herring. With onions." He chewed meditatively. "You know, Jim, this vacation is all good and well, but what about the place over there . . ." He jerked his head northward to indicate the general direction of the mansion.

"I know," Jim said. "We at least tried. . . ."

"Damn right. And there was something funny about the whole afternoon. You ever heard of a taxi driver not knowing his own neighborhood? That place looks about ten kilometers away, if that, and he couldn't find the god-damn road!"

"Yeah, there's something funny about it all right. Likely get our heads bashed in if we inquire too closely, I'm beginning to think," said the other. "Pass the *shoyu*."

Andy looked around for the soy sauce in its black iron-glaze container, then asked the man sitting near, "Could I have the purple, please?"

The man turned to Andy. He was a middle-aged Japanese with silver front teeth. "Ah, you know sushi very well!"

"So so," Andy said modestly.

"Do you like sushi?" the man asked, oblivious of the amounts the two young men were consuming.

"Very much," Andy grinned. "I eat all I can to make up for the times in America where it is unavailable."

"Ah, you are from America . . ."

"New York . . ."

"Ah, I would like to go there. I've always wanted to travel. You know? See the world. The Louvre and paintings. And also, I am interested in English painting, so maybe the Royal Gallery. And New York of course." He nudged Andy "There are many beautiful girls in New York?"

Andy grinned. "Prettier ones in California. Ask my brother."

"You are from California?" the man asked. "Hey, bring some sake for us!" The counterman rushed to obey. "How are the girls?"

Jim laughed. "As pretty as the pictures . . ."

Misunderstanding the stranger shook his head. "Nothing is as beautiful as Gainsborough." He grinned. "Though girls are warmer of course. You like girls, too?"

"Yep. All kinds."

"Ah, I love the big American girls." His hands demonstrated what part of them he particularly loved. "But the smell and the skin . . . only so so."

"Why?" asked Andy, sipping his beer, then biting at the piece of octopus he held in one hand.

"Japanese women. Such beautiful skin. You can sleep with a woman of ninety if she has good skin," the man said. "But if she has wrinkles, pores open? No, not even at twenty." He grinned shinily and sipped noisily at his tea. "*Uni* for the three of us here," he called, and the counterman replied with the customary "Hai!" and began putting the yellow sea-urchin gonads into little cones of black seaweed.

"My name is Hasegawa," the man said, producing the inevitable calling card. Jim and Andy followed suit.

"Midlaa-san, you are already president of a company?" Andy grinned. The beer was loosening his tongue. "Very small company . . ."

Hasegawa laughed. "It will be bigger someday. I was taught physiognimy reading by my father. I can tell."

"You are a physiognomist?" Jim asked. "I've always wanted to meet one."

Hasegawa laughed again as he munched at the sushi. Yellow paste oozed between his lips and he sucked it in. "No, no," he said, patting the air in front of him. "I sell agricultural products. More money in it. But I still remember what my father taught me. Excuse me for asking, but are you relatives, no?"

Jim stared at him sharply. Andy, tired and more affected by the beer, just nodded.

"I can tell," Hasegawa blithely continued. "I can read it on your faces. Come, I see you are finished. Let us go."

The two young foreigners were indeed finished. They signalled for the check which Hasegawa captured adroitly. Jim protested politely and Andy made protesting noises in his throat, but both knew the battle was lost from the beginning.

"*Gochan-desu!*" the three of them called out as they left. The big counterman called out something incomprehensible behind their backs.

"It is nothing. Nothing at all," Hasegawa hustled them out the door as they tried to thank him. "Come, I will show you what I mean about women's skin. Have you ever been to *toruko?* The best thing after a good meal."

Jim shook his head. Andy grinned and nodded quickly. "A Turkish bath is just what I need."

They walked several blocks through the tiny town. Down a dark alley they spotted a purple neon sign saying *toruko* and Hasegawa led them in that direction.

The entrance way was more elegant then the outside had led them to expect. Slippers were arranged in rows, backs to the door to allow for easy use. The floors shone with polished wood, and a semi-nautical theme of shells and fish dominated. A large net was hung from the ceiling with glass-bubble floats and dried starfish and blowfish caught in the rope folds. A scroll of cormorant fishing hung in an alcove.

The scroll and the decorations were obscured, in fact, unnoticed. *"Irasshaimase,"* the seven shrill female voices greeted the men as they entered. Except for one, the oldest who was dressed in an elaborate kimono, all the attendants were dressed alike; in cotton shorts and halters. The shorts were tight, exposing as much as possible of the warm brown skins.

Jim and Andy stopped and stared for a brief moment. Hasegawa urged them on. "Don't be shy, it's only a bath." He roared with laughter and the seven female voices joined in briefly.

"There are baths and there are baths," Andy answered. "And this appears to be a proper bath." He winked at one of the attendants and she giggled. "Not the kind Goemon was cooked in."

"I'm sure these beautiful ladies could bring even such a dangerous robber back to life," Hasegawa said, patting the nearest thigh.

Hasegawa was obviously a habitue of the place. They were led without questions to a room in the recesses of the bathhouse. Three of the attendants accompanied them while the hostess swayed off along the corridors, sliding the door closed behind her. The girls waited quietly, as

Hasegawa surveyed them and the two guests stared about them curiously.

Most of the room was occupied by a large tub. Plants had been set in pots along the walls, and the plaster was decorated by a hideous fresco of mermaids and tritons frolicking in the waves.

All three of the women wore white shorts and plain white cotton halters. Their exposed skin was smooth and unlined, their faces expressionless.

"Well," said Hasegawa. "A bath. Actually, I need the steam room, so I will leave you here for awhile. Please enjoy yourselves." He selected one of the women with his eyes and she followed him. Jim noticed that she was the oldest, but had an unlined face and erect carriage that promised great things. He looked at the two young women, wondering what was to come. It was one of the few instances when he felt he hadn't a clue as to the proper behavior.

Hasegawa disappeared along with his choice. The remaining two looked at the two young men with some trepidation. "You have bath, no?" one of them said in poor English notwithstanding the fact that both Jim and Andy had spoken in perfect Japanese not a minute before. *Gaijin* were *gaijin*, Jim mused, as Andy smiled broadly and said, "Of course. I'd love a bath."

The older one, with a red ribbon in her hair was Tsu. She had the appearance of a young housewife, and her attitude, at first, was brisk and impersonal. Hanako, the other, squinted shortsightedly at any object more than two meters away. It was obvious she normally wore glasses. Her hair was too short for a ribbon and curled enticingly over her forehead.

The two bath attendants stripped Jim and Andy, not allowing them to do the work for themselves. Their shirts came off while the women's red-chapped hands stroked their chests and bellies suggestively. Each woman then knelt before a man and they slowly and sensuously zipped down the men's flies.

Jim felt his cock hardening and Tsu who was undressing him lightly touched the bulge under his briefs. Slowly, with adequate care she unrolled the fabric down his thighs. Her head bent to her task and Jim could feel her warm breath on the tip of his member. For the briefest instant he thought he felt the bare flick of her tongue, too, but then the sensation was gone and only her breath panted heavily at the root of his desire. Notwithstanding his efforts the previous evening he had to fight the urge to push his cock into her waiting mouth and finish then and there. Only the vague notion he had of *toruke* etiquette stopped him.

He stepped out of his pants and she ran a sharp-nailed hand delicately up the inside of his thigh, ending with her thumb supporting his balls and her other fingers in the crack of his ass. Jim breathed heavily and stared at the red ribbon. Tsu grasped the root of his manhood gently and pulled downwards.

"You must wash," she said, "before entering the tub."

"Yes. Quite right. Yes," Jim breathed. He squatted by her side.

She raised a plastic bucket over head and poured a glittering stream over his shoulders and back. The water was hot and Jim winced. She repeated the action, squatting at his side. Jim could see that her halter, now that it was wet, was quite transparent. Dark nipples stared back at him through the translucent fabric. She rose and walked away from him, bending over to pick up the soap. Her white shorts were wet too and the moisture outlined the crease of her ass. The fabric tightened over her hips disclosing the fact that she wore no panties. Her mound bulged pinkly against the fabric.

Tsu started by soaping his back and shoulders. Her strong hands gradually descended to his buttocks, lathering the hair between his buns. Then she started rubbing his chest with the lather. Her full breasts, held tautly by the fabric of her bra rubbed deeply and silkily against his curved back. He could feel the nipples like two burning coals stroke his soapy skin. Her hands rubbed lower down his belly, and the backs of her hands stroked the upper side of his erect cock.

She lathered the nest of hairs from which his manhood sprung, and then with the utmost delicacy began soaping the rampant staff. Jim breathed heavily and his cock jerked involuntarily. He fought the sensation, biting his lips to bring pain. But the gently stroking hand, slicked by the soap continued its demands. With full movements of her hands and perfect control of her fingers Tsu milked his stiffened male teat. Jim's eyes glazed. He bent his head over his shoulder trying to capture her tongue, but she evaded his approach. His mouth caught at the red ribbon of her hair, and he spat it out.

At last he could stand it no more. Her turned to grab at her just as her urgently stroking hand squeezed the first spurt of his semen from the foam covered tip. Jim's hips jerked involuntarily then repeated the motion as spurts of his male fluid spattered the tiled floor.

"Now you are clean," Tsu said. "We can get into the bath." She rose to her feet with his hand in hers and stepped towards the bubble-covered water.

Andy watched Jim and Tsu with a hidden grin. Hanako was obviously less skilled than her older companion. She tried to emulate Tsu, but her touch was less sure, and her control of the situation less certain. She tried to avoid

Andy's groping hands, but ended up facing him, his hands stuck deep into her crotch as she tried milking him.

At first Andy was content to feel the mound. The small patch of crisp hairs excited him and he smiled at Hanako's face as she bent seriously at her task of "washing" him. Gradually he inserted his finger into her channel. At first it was only slightly moist and she squirmed uncomfortably. Soon however the male digit combined with the pressure of his palm on her clitoris eased the entry. She smiled back at him, swaying lightly with the motion of his finger, while not forgetting to stroke his vertical manroot.

Andy smiled back and inserted another finger. She swayed more rapidly now and her hole was looser, more open to his touch. He added a third and tried leaning forward to capture her mouth with his. She evaded his attempt with a giggle and soaped his cock harder. They were both breathing heavily now.

She made a futile stab at redirecting his attention by pouring water over him. He let the water run, then rose suddenly and poured a full bucket over her. She giggled uncontrollably. Her white clothes were practically transparent. Dark patches outlined her nipples and the V of her crotch. Some of the fabric caught between the plump lips of her cunt, leaving nothing to the imagination.

"You must get into the water with me and rub my back," Andy said. His erect cock was bobbing before him and she blinked, flicking her tongue out for a brief second as he stepped down into the tub.

The water had been scented with a bath oil, and small islands of suds rose with the movements of her hands. Hanako stepped in after him, still fully dressed. Andy turned his back to her and she began to rub it briskly, stirring the water as Jim and Tsu entered from the other end.

Andy leaned back and whispered, "Don't you find that lovely? Wouldn't you want some of that?" and he pointed at Jim's forward pointing cock.

Hanako stared unabashedly at Jim's erection that pointed straight at her before it sank beneath the waters. She giggled again and Andy turned to her. He crowded her against the corner of the tub and forced his mouth down on hers. She resisted for a moment, for propriety's sake, then yielded to his demanding tongue. He felt for her crotch again. Her hands went around his back and she allowed him full leave to explore her, hidden by the soapy waters. The water combined with the soapy oils did what they were supposed to do. She felt slick and warm inside as well as out. She squirmed delightedly as his fingers stroked her heated clit, and her eyes glazed as he sought and manipulated her fleshy lips and rather prominent clitoris. Andy wished they were out of the water. He would have liked to suck the tiny bud and test her reactions. He explored further and she made no objection, raising herself slightly in the water to facilitate the work of his hands. Another letch overcame him, and he explored further between her legs, finding the tiny muscular button of her rear. He stroked it for a while, not ignoring her cunt, wanting to make the sensation familiar for her ("if she's not used to it already," he added in a mental afternote. His cock jerked against her belly at the thought). She made no objection as he inserted one finger into her rectum, then another. The slippery water easing and soothing the access.

"Let me help you off your with your wet clothes," he whispered huskily. His voice was trembling with lust. They changed places and she settled herself on his thighs. He pulled off her shorts, then slipped open the halter catch and watched it float away in an island of foam. The fact that Jim and Tsu were watching from the other side of the bath excited Andy even more. He was sure Jim knew what he was up to, and could tell by the thrashing of legs under the water that Jim and Tsu were engaged in pleasures of their own. He raised Hanako in the water and probed for the little button with the broad tip of his cock. For a long moment he savored the sensation, then he pulled her ass to him, making his way slowly into the warm corrugated cavern.

Hanako shuddered as Andy's erection slid into her rectum. The gristly member was well lubricated by the soap in the water. His hands squeezed her slick small breasts and would have fastened painfully on the erect crinkled nipples but for the lack of friction. She twisted about to ease the pressure of the large prick up her and Andy buried his mouth in her neck, breathing deeply. The two soft buns of her bottom squeezed his shaft and floated weightlessly almost over his taut belly. One of his hands circled her belly and found the wet hairs of her cunt. He reached for her lower lips only to find her fingers already occupied with her own clitoris. Obligingly she made room for him and he felt the sweet nubbly flesh. Her own fingers plunged into her hole. With her other hand she sought out the shaft as it emerged from her behind. Squeezing her ass muscles she also stroked the base of his shaft with her fingers. Her eyes gradually closed as the pleasure of the moment overcame her.

Hasegawa knelt in the steam, his wiry body beaded with sweat. There was a flashing smile on his face. He was rocking backwards and forwards while staring through the one way mirror into the room next door. His cock was slipping in and out of the attendant's mouth. She was an elderly woman who usually catered to his needs, and her skin was as smooth and clear as a girl of twenty's. His movements speeded up and she prepared to receive her third mouthful of his male essence that night. His hands stroked the smooth nape of her neck, controlling the speed of her mouth movements.

"Ah, he is in her ass now. All the way in, I'm sure," he muttered. "So wonderful, the sight of his hairs washing against her bottom, like seaweed. Ag, he pushes again. And the other one is fucking in the cunt. Oh. So beautiful. I wonder which is which. Can't see under water. Suck harder. Ah, see, he is coming. It's spurting out, curling in the water like a cloud. And now the other one, too. They're still moving. Beautiful. Look at his hand in her cunt. Surely she is coming, too. I see her thighs trembling. How beautiful. Suck, suck! Ah, what a wonderful sight. Now me, too. Ahhhh"

He peered down at the head between his legs. She raised her face and opened her mouth. On her tongue rested the pearls of his offerings. Hasegawa smiled and slumped against the wall. She rose to fetch a cold towel to rub his face.

The tiny *minshuku* was warm and welcoming by the time they got back from the *toruko*.

"I hope they laid the *futon*," Jim mumbled sleepily.

They stopped at the entrance to their room and Andy could feel his heart racing. The belongings in their packs had been neatly taken out and laid on the bedding. Everything had been gone through with a thoroughness which indicated the searcher was looking for more than money.

The two edged nervously into the room, expecting the intruder to still be present. On the low table was a simple flower arrangement: a single clump of yellow rape flowers and a bare plum branch with tiny leaf buds not yet in full bloom, in a flat tray-like vase. A sharp toothpick held a visiting card pinned to the arrangement. On the card was a crude drawing of a thundercloud.

"Somehow," Andy said thoughtfully, "I think it is a mistake to have tried entering through the front door. Let's try another way."

"And another day," Jim agreed. "In other words, let's get the hell out of here."

# CHAPTER 8:

# THE GENERATION THAT THINKS YOUNG

"This is Jim. We are back in Gifu. Our trip was not a full success," Jim said to the red telephone. "Is Nakabe there?"

"No," Chieko said in alarm. "Why? What is the matter?"

"I have to see you right away! It's about the subject we discussed the previous time I was here."

"No, you can't. That is, of course, I can't . . ."

"Look, do you want her or not? I can't do anything without your help. I've got to talk to you."

"I'll tell you what. I'll meet you behind the shop later tonight, after closing time. No one is likely to interrupt."

"Right, that's exactly it!" A sudden idea bloomed in Jim's mind. Excitement gripped him. The shop. Of course. That might be the solution. "Listen, Chieko, do you have a dress like one Mineko wears?"

She laughed somewhat grimly. "Yes," she whispered, "yes, I do as a matter of fact. . . ."

"Wear it then. And your hair the way she does."

"Why? What are you doing?"

"Never mind," Jim said roughly. "Just do it. I'll see you there in twenty minutes."

He had been waiting for fifteen minutes by the time Chieko made her appearance. He sighed inwardly. No woman in his experience had ever been able to make an appointment on time. She unlocked the small rear door without speaking and motioned him inside. She led him by the light of the green emergency-door lighting to a small office, then through it to a *tatami* floored room beyond. Jim came up close behind her as she turned on the light and laid his palms on her ass.

Chieko turned to face him then pushed him away. "You have not yet performed our bargain," she said remotely. Her thin face regarded him cautiously.

"No," he admitted. "I need your help. Are you wearing something she likes?"

Chieko blushed, then nodded defiantly. "Yes," she almost whispered. "I wanted her so much, this was as close as I could get. . . ."

Jim grinned wolfishly. "Good. We have to get some equipment and set it up."

She aimed the small video camera as he turned on the lights. "Don't focus it too well," he warned. Chieko looked up in surprise. "Why not?"

"Turn it on," he said, not answering her question. He reached for her and pulled her away from the camera. His mouth covered hers and he clutched at her ass raising her on tiptoe.

Chieko responded fiercely to his kiss. Her tongue slid snakelike into his mouth, exploring the burning cavity and dueling with his own demanding tongue. One of his hands clenched on her buttocks and the slight pain built up the anticipation in her loins. The other time he had had her it was mildly painful, too, she recalled. His knee forced hers apart and his free left hand cupped her small breasts.

"Get down," Jim said, his dark face masklike. She fell to her knees, sliding her hands down his shirt, unbuttoning it, then zipping down his fly as she did so. She was conscious of the camera at her back, focusing on every movement. His cock sprung erect and she kissed the length, then popped the tip into her mouth. Jim jerked his hips forward convulsively a few times, then withdrew. He raised her head and smiled down at her. Perforce she returned his smile, trying to keep her face away from the camera. She trembled to think what would happen if the cassette were ever to fall into the wrong hands, and wondered what the strange foreigner whose taste was on her tongue intended.

"Down!" he commanded and she knelt on the *tatami* mats.

"Flip up your skirts!" She obeyed with alacrity, then, without any order from him, brought her fingers around her belly, stroking the prominent purse in full sight of the lens. Jim looked on approvingly. He dropped his pants and stepped out of them, then turned to bend over her. For a long delicious moment she could feel his hands stroking the taut golden skin of her behind. His fingers rested lightly on the soft small mounds, then he clenched his fingers and parted her excited and inflamed buns. She spread her knees to allow the camera full view of her ass. She wished she could enjoy the sight, too. The long slit

semihidden by her black hairs, the tiny starfish of her
anus, the warm tones of her skin.

Holding the buns apart with one hand, Jim leisurely
enjoyed the spectacle of Chieko's supine behind. He put
his left middle-finger to her mouth and she sucked at it
greedily. It was moist when he pulled it away. He placed
the finger on the tiny buttonhole of her anus. "Don't
move," he warned, his face away from the lens. "You'll
spoil the shot."

Chieko managed to control her involuntary reaction to
the touch on her rear hole. At first it was strange, but then
the sensation grew on her, a sensation of release from all
inhibitions as the male finger worked its way into her hot
muscular insides. She tried to suppress a small cry, then
decided not to try at all, and tiny gasps of pleasure excited
her lips as the questing finger worked its way into her
interior. Gradually her hips started undulating in time with
the man's fingers and she found herself pushing against
the male hand, intent on engulfing as much as she could
of the intrude in her anus. The little finger of Jim's hand
then found its way into her gaping slit, exposing the pink
interior as it darted in and out of her cunt.

Chieko's eyes closed and her head sank down to the
matting. She started jerking her hips forcefully back
against the tantalizing male hand, uttering low cries of
encouragement as she did so. Her hands turned to claws
tearing at the matting as her bodily demands took over.
She was unsurprised as Jim, without removing his hand
knelt behind her. His free hand pushed her buttocks down
to the floor after sliding a nearby handy *zabuton* sitting
pillow under her hips. He withdrew his fingers and she
automatically mewled a protest though she knew what was
coming.

His legs spread on either side of her hips, Jim grasped

his erect cock like a knife and crouched over her palpitating buttocks. He lowered himself, his jewel bag swinging freely over the open and inviting hillocks. The red plum-tip of his cock nudged the small hole, then started burying itself. He watched the head disappearing, then, once firmly lodged in Chieko's tiny muscular asshole, he released the shaft and pulled her buns as far apart as they would go. She moved uneasily for a while, then stilled as his shaft sank deeper into her. For a long delicious moment Jim paused in his actions. He wanted the camera to get a detailed view of what was going on. Then he crouched fully over her, his legs trembling with effort. One hand slipped over her belly and rubbed the erect nubbin of her cunt, with the other he supported some of his weight as he set to work to bugger the thin woman beneath him.

They worked together, her ass rising in time with the downward pile-drives of his cock into her body. He was conscious that she was fondling her own breasts, pinching them and squeezing the nipples as her desire rose in her. His strumming of her clitoris, and the fingers he dipped into her cunt were controlled by occasional urgent signals from her other hand as she forced him to adapt to her knees. Unconsciously she turned her head and he covered the view of her face with his and sought the pleasure of her lips. Unconsciously almost, she responded hungrily, sucking in his tongue and then seeking it out with her own.

They quickened towards a mutual climax, their joined hands strumming at her cunt, roughly punishing the waiting lips. His shaft flicked in and out of her lipless rear hole and her buttocks, crushed under the weight of his body and brushed by his pubic hairs, rebounded after each thrust. The juices boiled out of his balls, and feeling the jerking of his scrotum with her hands, Chieko joined with him in a frenzied storm of movement. The juices from his cock oozed in rich gobs along his pumping shaft, running down the moist hairs of her cunt. They collapsed together, his hips pinning hers to the mat, until finally his shrunken member was ejected from her ass by the muscular pressure natural to it.

Chieko rose and headed for the door. Suddenly she remembered. "The camera," she said in a low voice, not turning around.

"I'll cut this part off anyway," Jim said comfortably from his place on the floor. "I doubt I'll reach this far . . ."

After she had returned, drops of water still shining on her cunt hairs, she looked at him uneasily as he ejected the tape. "What are you going to do?" She nodded at the cassette.

"Give it to you to keep," he smiled, trying to ease her fears. "And make another one."

Chieko looked at him in puzzlement.

"Do you think you can convince Mineko to wear the same dress on a date with me? And can I have the key to the store?"

Understanding dawned on Chieko's face. "Yes, yes of course," she said. Her tone was thoughtful, and unconsciously the tip of her tongue wettened her lips.

"Tomorrow then. We'll stay in the town one more day."

"How are you?" Jim smiled broadly at Mineko. She smiled back and bowed slightly, affecting to ignore his open up-and-down study of her figure. He saw that Chieko had succeeded, by some mysterious means of her own, in getting Mineko to wear the same blouse and skirt she had worn the previous evening.

Taking her arm he led her off down into the shopping mall. "Shall we go to the 'Leopard' again?" he asked.

"Oh no," she smiled, "let's try somewhere else."

The place she led him to was dark-lit and quiet. Classical music played from hidden speakers and the walls were panelled in dark wood. Instead of tables there were dark booths lit by red-shrouded candles.

Jim grinned at her, divining her mind. "I see you know your way around . . ."

Mineko blushed slightly at the double entendre. From one of the dark booths they could hear a rustling and a stifled giggle. "I have never been here before," she confessed.

"And?" he prodded

"One of my friends told me . . ."

"And told you what we can do here. . . ?"

"No, no. But it is a good place where we can be by ourselves."

He laughed quietly and seated her in the booth, sliding into the surprisingly wide padded bench beside her. His hand rested casually on her thigh as he ordered, a mixed drink for her, whiskey for himself.

The drinks arrived as his hand was climbing higher up her thigh. His right hand followed, under her severe skirt this time. She shivered slightly, but made no objection to his exploration. His fingers crept up the inside of her thigh. She closed her eyes and began breathing heavily. He slid one finger under the elastic of her panties and she turned her face to his for a kiss. Her inner lips projected beyond the plumper outer ones and were wet to the touch. The fabric against which they were mashed was damp, too. He added a finger and sought for her clitoris among the damp hairs. Mineko shuddered at the touch and her tongue dove into his mouth in uncontrolled passion.

Jim kissed her cheek, then descended to her neck, nibbling at her ears, down to the V of her dress. She trembled again, allowing him to explore her cunt. He found the membrane that blocked entry and stroked it, hoping to widen the hole with his finger. With his free hand he reached for hers, and led her fingers to his fly. She fumbled at the zipper for a time, then managed to open his pants. His erect member sprang into the free air. Inexpertly she handled it, and Jim withdrew his face to allow her a glance at the machine that he hoped to bury in her soon. Her face betrayed nothing of her thoughts or emotions at the sight of the quivering fleshy column.

Mineko stroked his aroused member with a trembling hand. Jim breathed heavily, then attempted to raise her closest thigh over his. Her lips, both upper and lower, were wet with expectation. She shook her head in fierce negation, pulled away from him and clamped her thighs together. Jim tried to force the issue and she retreated sullenly to the back of the booth.

She laughed suddenly, hiding her mouth with her hand.

"What's so funny?" Jim raged.

"Nothing, really nothing, Jim-san," but the laughter still crinkled up the corners of her eyes.

"I'll take you home now," he said roughly. Silently, she regarded him out of dark-lashed eyes.

"Damn," he suddenly swore in English. Mineko jumped and he smiled at her soothingly. "I forgot something in Nakabe-san's office. Do you mind awfully if we pass by there? I must have it. Then I'll take you home to the dorm."

She nodded, relieved that his anger had not been aimed at her. *Gaijin,* even *nisei* which he appeared to be, were so unpredictable.

They entered the darkened store quietly, and Jim led her up the stairs to the tea room.

He noticed that Chieko had prepared the room as instructed. The camera was standing innocuously in one corner, its ready light hidden by tape. The remote control where it should be.

"Have you been here before?" he asked Mineko brightly.

"Yes, of course," she answered a shade nervously.

"Nakabe-san has kindly allowed me to have a key. I am working on some software for him," Jim said casually. They sat on the *zabuton* and Jim pulled her gently to him. She resisted his advances, pushing him away half-heartedly. He stroked her breasts through the flowery material of her blouse and bra, then leaned forward and kissed her deeply. Mineko responded ardently, clutching unskillfully at the iron-hard bulge in his pants. His hand groped behind her and he turned the camera on. His mind started counting. Mineko pulled away from him and took a deep breath. He laughed shakily at her, keeping her face in full view of the camera.

"I had better see you home," he whispered into her shoulder, then rose to his feet, pulling her after him. She stood reluctantly, puzzled at his lack of aggressiveness and passion. Jim bent down and kissed her deeply, then held her face back for the benefit of the camera while looking deeply into her eyes. He held the pose for awhile, pulling her to him in a demanding embrace. They swayed as they stood and Jim maneuvered her around so that her back was to the camera. He was at the end of the count and the "stop" button on the remote was clicked once again. He hoped briefly that the camera had been programmed properly. He had shown Chieko how to pre-program a fade out-and-in, but was not certain of her abilities. Bless

Japanese technology, he thought wryly as he withdrew from Mineko's arms and led her to the couch at the side of the room.

As he fondled the girl absently he felt his cock stiffen and thoughts of the delicious end to this night, so different from the previous time, percolated in his mind. Mineko allowed him to rub his hands across the bulge of her purse, outside her panties, and he gloated at the thought of the liberties soon to come. Her nipples felt hard and ready beneath the flowery fabric of her blouse, and her lips were moist with the flickering of their tongues as he pulled away from her.

"I must show you three things," Jim said.

"Three things?" she asked. There was a breathiness in her voice that he enjoyed hearing.

"Yes," he said, rising to his feet.

He opened the wall closet. Usually it contained tea-things, for the entertainment of the more traditional of the Nakabe Electronic Emporium's clients. Jim extracted a bottle of fine Osaka sake and two tiny cups. Mineko made a face. The expression turned to one of alarm as Jim quickly pulled out the *futon* bedding Chieko had placed there the same evening.

"No, no," Mineko said shaking her head violently and starting to rise.

"No, please," Jim stopped her with an upraised palm. "I am not going to force you, I promise. I just want to show you one other thing, and then, if you want, you can go."

The short girl subsided, still casting worried glances at the *futon* and then at Jim. He walked across the room and popped the cassette, inserted it in the playback machine, ran it back to the start of the cassette, and turned on the television.

"Do you know what this is?" Jim said stepping away from the screen.

"No," she said in puzzlement. "Why . . . ?"

"Look carefully," he said.

She sat quietly, a bit puzzled through the short section that had been filmed just moments ago with her and Jim. Her puzzlement turned to panic when the figure in the flowered print blouse fell to its knees in front of Jim.

"It's not me, no, it's not me . . ." she moaned in shock. Her eyes were glued hypnotically to the screen and she blushed but remained staring as the camera blurrily reproduced Jim's cock entering Chieko's asshole.

"The quality is blurred," he said, to distract her from looking too closely and realizing the substitution. "But I'm sure many men would like to see you like that."

His last words made her jerk away from the sight. "No. Not that. No. I will have to die. I will kill myself!"

He sat down beside her on the leather couch and stroked her shoulders. "Nonsense, my dear. Why should you do that?" Her shoulders trembled underneath his palms. "Look at me. See to what desperate measures you drove me? After all, I want us both to enjoy ourselves. And there is someone else, someone who loves you dearly. You could think of me as a go-between," he said coaxingly.

"A go-between?!" she responded, horrified yet amused.

"Yes," Jim replied. "Sometimes . . . sometimes a lover needs some help. I am helping that person."

Tears welled up again in her eyes. "But if that person . . . if that person . . . knows I'm . . . I'm . . . nnnnot a virgin . . ."

"To the contrary. Not only will that not matter, it is even better."

She shook her head in confusion. Gently he kissed her

neck then pushed her back onto the bed. She sank slowly backwards and made only token protest when he pulled her down onto the waiting *futon* and began unbuttoning her flowery blouse.

"Will I have to . . ." she waved a hand weakly at the screen where she could see Jim's cock jerking spasmodically into what she thought, but could not understand, was her own bottom.

"Only when you want to," Jim said soothingly.

She squeezed her eyes tightly shut. Without a word he stood up and her eyes snapped open. He stood in the middle of the spread *futon* and stripped his clothes off matter-of-factly. His brown cock was semierect and she stared at it in horrified fascination. Gradually another emotion emerged on her panicked face. A gleam appeared in her eyes and she looked more fully at the thickening member. Her lips parted and her gaze flickered nervously from the cock to the floor then back again. Her hands, that had been clenched before her chest gradually fell to her lap.

Jim lay back on the futon. He stroked his erection lightly, his palm running the full length of the shaft. Mineko looked at it openly now, with an attentive expression. Jim said nothing. Drawn by invisible strings she rose to her feet. Then, as if an irrevocable decision had been made, her hand flew to the buttons on her blouse. Hurriedly she stripped off her clothes. Jim had a bare glimpse of her full smooth body, a flash of the dark triangle at the base of her belly and the full breasts that bounced as she moved, and then she was under the light cover on the mattress.

Leisurely he rose and crawled in with her. He pulled her full frame to his. There was no reluctance on her part, only curiosity and a growing sense of pleasure. Jim kissed her deeply, exploring her mouth with his tongue. She glued her body to his, seeking as much contact as she could. He pulled her soft hand to his cock and she responded with alacrity. Clumsily, but with increasing confidence she stroked the shaft, marvelling at the silky texture, at the looseness of the skin over the blazing metal hard interior.

Jim lowered his head and sucked at her full breasts, cramming as much as he could of one into his mouth while squeezing the other. She whispered something brokenly. He reversed his actions and could feel the dampness on the full mound his mouth had just left. She urged him on, pushing as much of herself into him as she could. His free hand sneaked between their bodies and stroked the smooth soft cunt hairs, then dipped lower into the split. She was damp, her thighs completely parted. His fingers found the tiny opening and he enlarged it somewhat with his fingers, which were blocked in their actions by the virginal membrane. He kissed the bottom side of each full breast then started sliding himself downwards, leaving a trail of tiny wet kisses on her skin.

"Now!" she whispered fiercely. "Now. Now before I change my mind. Do it now!"

Jim looked up in surprise and some disappointment. The desire for a taste of her fresh young cunt was fully upon him and he did not like being frustrated in his desires. But her hands were digging painfully into his shoulders and she tugged him up to her mouth again. Almost forcing him she rolled herself under his frame and spread her legs. Her mouth clamped to his and her thighs parted as widely as they could. Then her hand clawed at his back and he butted forward with his hips, the blunt spearhead of his cock searching out the tiny hole. Mineko aided him as best she could while her mouth sucked hungrily at his. In a few seconds Jim found himself lodged in the wet entrance to her virginal cunt. She heaved her hips up, lost

the promised treat, then found it agin in frantic entreaty.
His hands roved over her body, enjoying the tremors they
aroused. Soon he was lodged in her again. He pushed
forward again, spreading the reluctant but wet lips with
the flanges of his cock-head. She cried out into his mouth,
reluctant to leave his tongue. Jim forced forward again.
Her eyes widened, but she pulled at him again, urging
him on with purring sounds that sent vibrations through
his mouth and skull to the depths of his balls.

He felt the thin membrane tearing against the spongy
skin of his knob and he clutched her to his own body in
triumphant delight. She did not pull back notwithstanding
the pain. Instead her hips and hands clutched at him, forcing more of his maleness into her. His mouth sought hers
again and she responded with a hungry kiss, as if glad to
absolve him and herself of the burden of her virginity.

She gasped again and again but would not relinquish
her hold on him as his prick made its burning way up her
vaginal channel. He rested for a short while, embedded
fully in her. Instinctively, answering the natural call of
her body, she started moving her hips. Jim pinned her to
the ground and smiled down at her round face. He caught
one of her hands in his and helped her explore the junction
of their bodies. Their pubic hairs were mashed together
and he twisted their joined fingers through the mossy forest. Then he touched the lips distended around his maleness. She sucked in a hiss of air at the burning sensation
that came from the bruised flesh, then explored the disten-
tion, smiling triumphantly. Finally he led her to touch the
part of his shaft that was not embedded in her, and the
soft pulsing hair bag beneath.

"Leave your hand there," he whispered, and began
moving in and out of her.

"Jim-san, this is so exciting, so wonderful. I was such

a fool," she whispered into his ear. "I so wanted you. So much. So much," she gasped brokenly as she felt the pleasure of his penetration overcome the slight pain.

"Squeeze the shaft with your hand," he whispered and she obeyed with alacrity.

"It is soooo big," she wailed, touching his cock and balls with a frenzy that threatened to cause unintended damage.

Lost in his pleasure Jim paid no attention, the speed of his thrusts increasing. He watched her face carefully, intent on bringing about her climax. She was soon reacting happily to his thrusts, trying to change the position of her hips to accommodate him and stimulate herself. Her knees rose higher until she could cross her ankles over his heaving back, throwing off the light cover as she did so. For a single rational moment Jim was sorry he did not have the camera going, then the thought slipped beneath the level of consciousness and he was lost in the pleasure of her tight grasping hole.

Mineko squealed once as her first orgasm overtook her. Shudders ran through her body and she voiced wordless sounds that were barely hidden by Jim's shoulder. Again and again she clutched him convulsively to her slick body. Jim responded by grinding his hips in a circular motion into her, stroking and raising her butt as he did so. She panted heavily and he raised his torso, intending to change their position, but she fought him back into place. He started thrusting into her again and she smiled gratefully, then closed her eyes and sought his mouth with hers.

This time Jim pulled out almost to the tip, then started a corkscrew motion that sent her quickly into a frenzy. She jerked at his body hungrily, practically throwing both of them off the *futon*. He eagerly nibbled at the skin of her shoulders and neck, arching his back to reach the prominent pink nipples of her flushed breasts. Again she cried out, her eyes closed, as she reached her orgasm. Jim did not stop. He pistoned his aroused cock in and out of her sweet flesh. His bags slapped against the rounds of her ass and sweat dripped off him with his efforts.

A rush started from his balls, and he was poised like a wave, his pubis jammed against hers. The length of his cock forced one last shriek out of her as a flood of white cream erupted from his cock and innundated her interior. His final spasms were less spectacular, but still Mineko peered at Jim in wonder, pulling at his cock and ass to force more of his maleness inside her. She felt the thick flood of spunk roll out from between the shaft and her own lower lips, and another thrill shook her body. Jim opened his own eyes, saw she was in the midst of still another orgasm, and lowered his mouth to hers.

A long time later he rolled off her smooth body. She held on to him, cradling her head on his sweaty chest.

"Why did you laugh at me? In the cafe?" he asked, not looking at her.

She stirred on his chest and Jim was conscious that she was studying the lines of his face.

"Not at you," she said quietly. "At myself. For being such a fool. I wanted you so much . . ."

Jim grunted doubtfully, then remembered Chieko. There was still another act to the drama.

He groped under the nearby sofa for the signal caller that he knew would bring Chieko running. Soon he heard footsteps rapidly climbing the stairs. Mineko half rose from the bed when the door opened and Chieko stepped in. The light blanket fell from her shoulders exposing her full breasts which bounced with the rapidity of her motion. She clutched hastily at the cover just as Jim pulled her back onto the *futon*.

"Relax," he murmured into her ear. "There is nothing to be afraid of. Nothing to worry about."

Mineko started to say something, then her eyes widened as Chieko, with a couple of swift strides shook off her shoes and knelt by the side of the bed. She put her palms flat on Mineko's pink cheeks and gazed deeply into the troubled girl's eyes.

"Darling Mineko," she whispered hoarsely, "you must not be afraid of me." Her red-painted mouth descended onto Mineko's. Her tongue thrust forward, not admitting to any refusal. For a brief moment Mineko seemed to be trying to make up her mind, then the tension in her lips broke. They opened and she passively admitted Chieko's exploring lingual scout into the portals of her mouth.

Jim supported both women as the kiss went on and on. At first there was no movement. Then Chieko started licking Mineko's mouth, her lips crushing those of the passive young girl's. She started moaning, her mouth still glued to the object of her infatuation. Mineko barely responded, but the renewed flush of her neck and breast, and here quickened breathing showed that the embrace was not at all against her wishes.

Chieko finally broke free. Her hands slid to Mineko's shoulders,. Her eyes gazed deeply into the other girl's eyes, completely ignoring Jim.

"You are so sweet, so beautiful," she said brokenly. "So beautiful. I love you so much."

Mineko's heavy eyelashes slid down over her eyes. She drew a silent breath Jim could feel against his bare chest, but not hear.

Not drawing her eyes from the bare-torsoed girl on the bedding, Chieko rose and began undressing. Her white polka-dotted dress was soon followed by a filmy shift. She wore no nylons or bra. For a moment she posed before the object of her adoration. Her thin body had filled out somewhat from the days in Tokyo, but she was still slim. She ran her hands over her flat stomach, toyed with her own breasts while smiling secretly, then dipped into the bush at the juncture of her legs.

She returned and knelt with one knee on the *futon*. In that position, with one knee raised, Minkeo could see the depths of the other woman's slit. The bulging outer lips fascinated her, and for the first time she wondered secretly what a kiss there would taste like. With a steady pull Chieko divested Mineko of the blanket. Reluctantly almost, her half-closed eyes heavily shadowed, the other girl let go of her covering. Chieko regarded her prize for a long delicious moment. Mineko was everything she had imagined. Her figure was full and soft, her breasts large and promising. The sparse hairs on her mound meant less interference and greater contact. At the thought of the tiny half seen slit Chieko's mouth watered. She knelt on the quilt and gently but firmly pried the plump golden thighs apart. Mineko looked on. The older girl's head dipped. Without touching it she examined the ragged slit. There was a tiny smear of fresh blood. Chieko's own blood pounded in her head at the sight, awakening feelings of protectiveness, rage at the despoiling male, while, paradoxically, glee at the pain Mineko had suffered. She recalled that Jim's cock had been the first into here as well, and the memory of the delight and slight pain moved her to action. Her head descended, her nose leading her to the delightful scent of newly awakened womanhood, and her tongue leaped out to taste the juices of her love.

Mineko watched the incomprehension as Chieko's head, her tight hair bound in a bun, descended between her legs. She was uneasy, feeling Chieko was examining her for something, still not knowing what was really happening.

By nature she was passive, allowing other people to shape her life. Now Chieko, a married woman she had been friendly with for months, was inspecting her newly torn vagina.

A sensation she had never felt before suddenly invaded her loins. It spread from the tiny nubbin that was the seat of her pleasure, one she had rubbed often enough, one bruised by Jim's assault, to the rest of her belly. The pleasure was so intense, so all-encompassing she felt helpless in the onrush. Suddenly she knew what it was as Chieko's experienced mouth explored the recesses of her cunt. Involuntarily Mineko cried out loudly. Her thighs fell apart to permit the magical member more access to her sensitive tissues. The sensation changed, intensified, as Chieko parted her lips, sucking in clitoris and as much of the girl's lower lips as she could encompass. Lightly, but with growing determination and pressure, she sucked the delightful morsel, even touching it lightly with her teeth as the faint flavor of virginal blood accompanied the honey taste of Mineko's fresh cunt.

# CHAPTER 9:

# SILENT IS THE NIGHT

They were deep in the mountains by the time they got off the bus from Gifu City. The small town they had stopped in bore the sulphurous smells of natural springs: its major attraction. Traces of winter snow still lay on the ground and the murmur and chuckle of melting water accompanied every activity. The *minshuku* they chose was a large one, full of farmers and local tourists out for a good time. They were lucky, the maid who showed them to their tiny room said, to find a room at all. There were several tour groups of farmers' cooperatives and a university club staying the night. Elderly and not so elderly men and women were bustling up and down the corridors in *yukata* and slippers. Most were heading to or from the baths. Elderly men in faces red with drink and farm work and white long johns chattered amiably as they climbed up and down the steep wooden stairs.

"Lively place," Andy chuckled.

"Yeah," Jim said wryly, poking his head out the door, and pulling it in again like a turtle as a coterie of fat elderly housewives, well into drink and good cheer rolled by. They ogled the young man unashamedly. "Plenty of drunks dropping in to our room during the night, too."

"Coming for a bath?" Andy said idly as he tied the *yukata* sash behind him with some effort.

"No. Don't think I can put up with any drunks just right now. I'm beat."

Andy grinned at his darker brother as he headed for the door. "Nakabe's wife really took it out of you, eh?"

"If you only knew," Jim responded. His thoughts were on Mineko as he lay back on the spread *futon*. The door popped open as he was about to drop off and a drunken voice called out loudly for "Yamamura!" Jim sat up and explained there was no Yamamura there. The red drunken face disappeared, and Jim fell into a restless doze in which Mineko and Chieko teased him alternatively, flicking his cock between them, never allowing him a chance to reach an orgasm.

He awoke to the sounds of revelry in some far off room of the inn. His cock felt as hard as iron, jutting out before him and unwilling to let him rest. He also had a powerful thirst. The latter problem was easily assuaged. He clicked open the tiny fridge in the room and extracted a can of Asahi beer. The fridge chuckled to itself, a tiny pilot light glowed, and he knew another charge was being added to his bill. He gulped the beer barely tasting the brew. Peering downwards somewhat blearily, he decided the only way to rid himself of the thing, in the absence of a willing nubile female, was a bath. Preferably after a cold shower. He considered dressing in pants to hide the bulge. The thing was positively unnatural. Shrugging mentally and tying his sash tighter to support the swaying rod, he grabbed a large towel and left the room.

It was quite late by now and Jim wondered what had

happened to Andy. The corridors had been darkened, but
the late hour did not seem to limit the sounds of revelry
in any way, though there were fewer casual strollers in
the corridor.

Dazed by the sleep and the beer Jim leaned for support
against a door he had thought locked. It swung open to
the sounds of liquid sex. Two bodies were entwined on a
*futon* in the middle of the room. The muscular buttocks
of a middle-aged, rather plump man were bobbing uncontrollably over the splayed thighs of a well-endowed Japanese woman. Her head was thrown back and her mouth
open. His head was covering one of her full flattened
breasts. His hands were under her buttocks, while hers
were around his shoulder egging him on. As Jim watched
a powerful spasm shook both bodies. The smooth rhythm
of the man's buttocks trebled in frequency and the woman
squealed aloud. The man's cock jerked again and again
and large drops of pearly liquid were squeezed from her
lips and ran, moistening his shaft.

Jim stared hypnotized at the sight. His mouth opened
and he struggled for air. A wave of lust seemed to emanate
from the couple on the bedding. The smell—sex and
sperm and female essence, and above all, the musk of sex
consummated—made Jim take a step towards them when
the couple noticed his presence. Reason took Jim by the
scruff of the neck and flung him out of the room. He did
not stay to hear the man's words, which barely impinged
on his consciousness as he lost himself in the maze of
corridors. He finally reached the door to his room.
Trembling, he tried to insert his key into the door. It
would not turn the lock. He struggled with the door only
to discover it was not locked in the first place. Jim stepped
in, expecting to see Andy, sodden no doubt, lying on his
*futon*. Instead, he saw the reclining form of a woman, her

loose shoulder-length brown hair sweeping the cushion. Her eyes were closed and one of her hands was inserted between her legs, the *yukata* barely hiding the busy activity of her fingers. Jim's forgotten erection twitched, bringing itself back to his notice. The woman opened her eyes to see the young man towering over her.

Jim was too dazed with lust to control himself. The woman half rose out of the bedclothes. Her hair hung over her eyes and one full white breast had popped out of the loose *yukata*. He stumbled forward and fell onto her. For a moment she froze. The momentary pause gave Jim a chance to assert himself. He grasped the full tit and bore her backwards. She started to shriek and his hungry mouth closed over hers. Her hands came into action. She tried to push his body off her chest, but her arms were no match for his weight. The struggle disarranged the bed clothes still further. Jim could feel her smooth limbs working under his and the sensation sent him into a frenzy. He pulled her hands savagely aside, slipped off the *obi* around his middle, and looped the length of cloth around her hands. His cock was like a bar of molten iron and his eyes were blazing rabidly. He slipped her over and pulled the *yukata* off her. Full rounded pale moons were exposed to his gaze. He laid his full weight upon her, and her scream was muffled by the hard pillow, the sounds drowned in the calls of the party goers outside. He forced his knees between hers and his hot cock rested along the crack of her ass. His hands were clutching at her full breasts, mauling the soft pillowy mounds while she sobbed for breath.

The woman tried to jerk him off and Jim utilized the opportunity to pull her to her knees. Suddenly the fight seemed to go out of her. Her arching back sagged and Jim could hear her panting beneath him. He felt a moment of pity, hardly believing that it was he who was performing the act, then the urgencies of his body overtook him again. He stroked her hips and then inserted a finger in the crack of her ass. She buried her face in the pillow, allowing him full play to his curiosity.

Jim examined her behind in the dim light. The crack of her ass was smooth and hairless. The lips of her cunt, hidden in front by a full growth of hair, were now naked to his gaze. He inserted a finger, as gently as he could under the circumstances, between the soft lips. She sucked in a breath and her behind twitched uncomfortably. He twisted one finger about in the delightful hole, then hurriedly added a second and then a third. He did not know how long he could contain himself. The tip of his cock was sparkling with the preliminary drops of transparent fluid.

His hands withdrew from her cunt and hips and he grasped her hanging fat tits firmly. Jim's hips jerked forward without his conscious volition and he felt the long shaft sink itself deeply into the woman's wet cunt.

He fucked her furiously, the slaps of his belly against her upraised ass sounding like gunshots. She bore his onslaught patiently at first, then found herself slipping into rhythm with him. Her own emotions were aroused. Her fury against the man raping her did not abate, but her body seemed to lead a life of its own. She moaned, then, ashamed of her seeming compliance, hid her face in the cushion. The thrusts quickened and she could feel the slap of his balls against her thighs. She wondered, her mind off on a tangent, if the blows hurt him. For a moment she thought she would free her hands and squeeze him to a painful end. But her body pleaded with her "No, no, not yet," and then the rising tide of her own helpless lust swept her along.

Above her Jim was breathing stertorously. His face was contorted and there was nothing in his mind but the need to force himself deeper and deeper into the helpless mounds of sweet-smelling ass before him. Dribble fell unnoticed from his lips and his hands clenched, unnoticed by either of the fuckers, on her generous hips. She shoved her ass back at him, jerking and shaking her thighs uncontrollably. She tried to urge him on as her orgasm struck her. The power of her muscular rictus raised her from her knees as she jerked back against the thick cock imprisoned in her now-willing cunt. She grunted and raised them both in the air, her cunt clutching at the flame that penetrated her from his flesh-root. Waves of perverse pleasure racked her body and she screamed into the pillow.

As she collapsed Jim's cock spewed forth its glutinous juices. He shook at her entrance as a terrier shakes a rat. The red inflamed head jerked out of her opening and spewed sticky come over the rounded smooth hills of her ass. It dribbled down the crack between and beaded her skin and the quilts as he collapsed on top of her. They lay quietly in the aftermath of their climaxes. Jim did not know what to do. Stroking her hair, kissing her, any of the little things he normally did seemed ridiculous under the circumstances.

He rolled off her and lay on his back. Her face was still hidden from him. They were both breathing heavily.

"You could at least have said 'thank you,' " she said, her voice muffled by the pillow.

"I am very sorry. I don't know what . . . what I was doing."

"No." She said in a tired voice. "I was going to kill you, before, when I was still coherent." She turned to face him. "Now I don't know what I feel. Dirty. Used. But there was something . . . something that happened . . ."

Jim shyly kissed her shoulder. At first it trembled away from him, but then she nestled closer.

"My friends might return any minute," she said.

"Haven't you been outside?" he asked in surprise. "Everyone is drunk and behaving strangely. . . ."

"Imagine!" she exclaimed, raising her head from the pillow. "Well I never!! That is very strange indeed."

Jim kissed her shoulder again, then the pillar of her neck. She turned to face him and he kissed her lips, bruised by his earlier brutality, with a gentle touch.

"Is that an apology?" she demanded in a strong country accent.

"Yes," he said humbly.

"It is not sufficient," she said demandingly. "Do it again." She held out one full rounded breast and he kissed it gently. The nipple jutted out perkily, slipping between his lips, then was withdrawn again.

"I could go to the police you know," she said.

"I know," he said with a half-hidden tremor.

"You must apologize. Often. Where and how I tell you."

He nodded in the dimness.

"Stand up," she said.

Jim obeyed with alacrity, though the room was cold on his bare flesh. A sudden light lanced through the dark as she switched on the flashlight that is standard equipment in all inn rooms in Japan. The light spotted parts of his anatomy, lingering over his crotch and face.

"Quite handsome," the woman remarked for both their benefits. "But you're not erect."

"Ah well, of course . . ."

"Let me see you," she said.

"Now? So soon?"

"I want a proper apology," she muttered. "Yes, of course now."

Jim started stroking his sticky semi-soft shaft. Reluctantly it began growing as he found precisely the right spots in his own anatomy. She left the light on him until he was fully erect.

"Nice," she commented. "Now come and apologize again."

He knelt beside her and presented his cock which she brushed impatiently away. "No. With your mouth. A proper apology."

He started with light kisses, fleetingly touching her cooling sweat bedecked skin and working his way downwards. He grazed the forest of damp hairs at the base of her belly and worked downwards. She raised her head on a hard pillow and watched him between her breasts. The skin of her belly and thighs was particularly sensitive he found out. Every time he applied his tongue to her there, she quivered. The closer he approached her lips, the longer the quivers lasted. At last the tip of his tongue licked out and touched her inflamed pink clitoris which stuck out slightly from under its protective skin hood. She trembled violently and pulled her knees up.

Jim tried again, tasting their mingled juices on his tongue. Then after wiping her hurriedly with a corner of the covering, he applied his mouth in full earnest to her cunt. She shivered and moaned loudly, clutching at his head and ears, heedless of the pain she was inflicting. His tongue, lips, and teeth worked together, searching out the folds of her pussy, treating them all with sharp suckings and lickings.

"The other hole, too," she demanded in a hoarse whisper.

"What?" he asked, his mouth muffled by the fur of her cunt.

In response she raised her feet and brought them to her head, her knees touching the flat mound of her breasts. "The little hole beneath, too."

Reluctantly Jim's tongue probed the tiny anal button. It smelled fully of her female juices. She had apparently washed before retiring, but now the mingled juices of her cunt and his cock had run down and moistened the tiny hole. Emboldened by his first try, he licked out again. Her frame shuddered in response.

She rolled him onto his back and straddled him, then grasped his softening cock in her fist. Shaking it roughly, she looked at the tube of flesh curiously, then bent forward for a more thorough examination.

"So this is what causes so much trouble in the world." She shook his cock roughly. "And so much pleasure." She stroked the bottom of the shaft with a heavy thumb.

She raised her backside from his hips and inched forward until her cunt was directly above his hapless face.

"Would you like to eat me again?" she asked. Her fingers pulled the outer lips apart, exposing the soft moist red membranes inside.

Not answering he raised his head and his tongue stuck out. He licked the length of her lips, not neglecting her fingers, then probed at the depths of her exposed hole.

"Not yet," she said huskily. "Just answer the question!"

"Yes," he said.

"You would really want to do that?"

"Yes, I'd love to," he said sincerely. The smell of her cunt was intoxicating him and he longed to probe her with his tongue and lips.

She peered down at him over her breasts. "That is strange," she murmured to herself. Then the tone of command in her voice hardened. "Lick my other hole first then."

"What . . ." he started to say.

"Lick my other hole again then," she commanded.

Somehow he knew that there was no threat in her words. He could refuse, and she would be disappointed, that would be all. And he didn't really want to do that, though she had just recently come from her bath. But the commanding tone was compelling. He found himself licking at the previously moistened muscular hole. Tentatively at first, then urged on by her voice, he took to his work seriously. His tongue probed at her anus, trying to force its way in to the waiting hole. She bent forward uncomfortably, her head above his to view the operation, then started moving her hips in time to his licks.

At last she pulled away. Her face was streaked with sweat, and he knew that only some of it was from the effort of squatting over his face. "Now my cunt. From behind," she whispered and rolled into a crouch, exposing her ass and the prominent purse to his gaze and tongue.

The whisper was a command, but first he felt he needed to finish her other command. His tongue licked and probed at her anus again, then gradually started working its way down to the extruded lips that were covered with downy black hair.

"Suck it!" she commanded, and her frame shuddered with orgasm as he obeyed, sucking in the delicate folds and ingesting their moisture. He moved his head as she shook frantically, his nose butting at her rear entrance and adding to her pleasure.

She rocked against him for some time before falling forward onto the *futon*.

"That was nice," she said huskily over her shoulder. He crawled over to her side. She looked down the length of his brown body. A new idea occurred to her. Rising, she walked to the armchair in the enclosed veranda. She stood on one foot and raised the other, then pulled her cunt open.

"Come here," she said. "Fuck me standing up."

Jim bent his legs to insert himself into her waiting cunt. She grasped the shaft cruelly and massaged her inflamed tissues. Jim purpled with effort, but the spell of her command was still upon him. When she had had enough she released his erection and bent forward. He stood at her side and shoved until he was lodged firmly up her.

"Fuck me until I say you can stop," she ordered. He jogged into her as she reached forward to open the *shoji* and peer down into the street below. Casually she directed his movements, stopping only to tremble with her climaxes, squeezing his shaft in warning whenever, in her opinion, he threatened to come.

When she had had enough, when her leg was trembling with fatigue she ordered him out of her. His erection glistened in the moonlight and he stared at her with a dumb questioning look.

"Masturbate yourself to a climax," she ordered coolly.

Haplessly the young man obeyed, still under the spell of her command. His breathing hoarsened, the movements of his fist along the shaft quickened, and suddenly a spurt of white semen leaped out of the shaft and besprinkled the floor. Another followed immediately, and then a third.

Jim opened his eyes and looked at the woman again. Her eyes were misty and she peered intently at the gobs that had emerged from his now drooping cock. But her voice was still steady and commanding.

"Clean up after yourself, then leave," she ordered him.

Jim found some tissues and cleaned up, slipped on his *yukata* and left the room. Behind him the woman relaxed deeply into her *futon*. She smiled sleepily as the door closed behind the young man.

# CHAPTER 10:

# STRIPPED FOR ACTION

Andy sat down on the small plastic stool in the steamy room and washed himself thoroughly while dreamily contemplating the lush vegetation planted in pots around the large bath hall's periphery.

"Uus!" a loud voice said in his ear and he almost spilled the contents of a hot bucket over his feet. Andy turned slowly to see an eager young face peering at him. For a moment he could not remember where he had seen it before, and then the something swam into focus.

"Tamura? Is that really you?"

"*Senpai!* I am pleased to see you here! Just in time for the party, too!"

Andy shook his head. "Party? Ah, yes, of course!" Things became suddenly clearer as Tamura turned and urged him to join the group, announcing loudly, "Here is Senior Midlaa! He is joining the party!"

Andy sank himself into the warm water. The names

behind some of the faces returned. Ito, who had been small and chubby, was now large and tubby. Sakurai's pimples had dried up. Ito . . . The boy with the strange name, what was it . . . Sue', that's it. Members of the Economics Club he had been a member of. And now he was an Old Boy. Better act the part then. "So," he said, mock severely. "You're all seniors now. Congratulations."

They thanked him, grinning. They were graduates now, about to embark upon careers, but the ties they had made as members of a prestigious university club would serve them the rest of their lives. And Andy, as a senior member, a *senpai,* was part of their world as well.

They gossiped about the club, about other seniors, both older and younger than Andy. A heavy body heaved itself into the pool, turned to Andy and grinned. "Watching over the youngsters, are you?"

Andy grinned back. "How are you Matsumura?"

"Matsumura *shacho,* please!" the other bowed in the tub.

"Already?" Andy raised his eyebrows.

"Old man gave me one of his companies."

"That's great. How's it going?"

"Tiring. But wonderful. Came for the party did you?"

Andy forbore an explanation, anxious to explore possibilities with his friend. "Who's collecting contributions to the party?" he asked Matsumura in a whisper as they dressed. He hoped he had enough cash: being a respected alumnus tended to be expensive.

"I'll take care of it. Don't worry. Come to the Ho-o lounge at eight. Lots of fun."

By the time dinner was over, Andy's inhibitions were gone. Seated in *yukata* at long tables piled with food, the members, past and present of the club, had regaled one

another with songs and toasts. The freshmen had been
required to drink to everyone's health, and had then been
catechized on the club's aims. Older former members had
given long speeches ending with contributions to the club's
treasury. Beer and sake had washed down plates of *sashimi*,
grilled fish, soup, seaweed salads, meats, noodles,
thin slices of butter with raisins embedded in them, and
assorted other tidbits. The older former members excused
themselves, to party elsewhere, as Andy knew. The party
grew rowdier. Men sprawled on the soft mats, chatting,
smoking, nibbling and drinking, always drinking. A freshmen,
sodden by four large beers and sake chasers forced
on him by his seniors was led out by his friends. Another
sprawled in the corner, dead to the world. Others, more
experienced, drank again and again with their seniors as
they circulated among the low tables.

Matsumura rose and clapped his hands. "This is the
final party of the year, when you bid farewell to the former
officers of the club. Get up, gentlemen, let everyone see
you. There. These young men have led our club proudly
through the year. They are now about to retire, to become
Old Boys, like me and our *gaijin* member, Midlaa-san.
This does not cut their ties with the club, as you can see,
it is merely the step into a new world. However, we have
decided to arrange some special entertainment for them,
and for us of course." He laughed uproariously and beckoned at the door. The female figure stepped through and
slid the door to behind her. She slipped a cassette into the
machine in the corner, and languidly began dancing to a
folk melody, swaying gracefully as some of the young
men crowded around her.

"The Old Boys would provide some of that old-fash-
ioned stuff," grumped one of the younger members of the
club as he edged forward with the rest.

Andy was not particularly fond of traditional dancing, and he watched from behind, still sipping at a cup of lukewarm sake, wondering whether he should seek his bed. He blinked suddenly, and craned forward as did all the other spectators. With a lithe movement the dancer had shrugged one shoulder out of her gay dancing kimono. The heavy cloth fell down, exposing a full rounded breast to the youngsters' gaping eyes. She languorously shrugged into the garment again. A few more steps, and the other lapel fell away, exposing her other breast. The dancer fondled it a moment as she raised her clothes again. The music gradually changed, the tempo speeding up as the club members became glued to her movements. She suddenly slid her foot forward in a long step, posing for a moment, the entire length of her naked leg exposed to the crotch,

With unhurried movements, her hands caressing her body, the stripper divested herself of her brocade *obi* sash, the opening exposing her body for flashes of browned flesh. The younger members of the club were mesmerized and Andy licked his lips. Bulges appeared under every *yukata*. The stripper turned dramatically and posed, her *kimono* held open like wings. The music changed to a Western dance tune and she dropped the heavy garment. For a moment they could see the length of her body. The perfect dancer's torso topped slim legs. Her full ass was barely hidden by a gauzy veil wrapped around her hips. She turned and pulled the veil up to cover herself, then started a languid dance, brushing the tips of the fabric against the mesmerized boys' faces. The music grew slower. The dancer sank to the floor and contorted her body, her charms barely hidden by the transparent pink fabric. She sat on the floor, one leg extended to her side, the other folded beneath her, a foot hiding the entrance to paradise. The top of her small bush was fully visible. She beckoned to one of the freshmen. Hypnotized, he followed the pointing finger, sinking to *seiza* before her. With a quick movement she extended her folded leg and whisked the veil away from her groin. Her beckoning finger led him on until his nose was almost between her thighs.

She laughed lightly, and the sound of her laughter broke the spell. The boy broke away, his face suffused with red. For a moment she held her pose. Her legs wide open, she held the lips of her cunt agape with the fingers of her left hand while stroking them with her right. A collective sigh rose from her audience. She laughed again, rose lithely and was through the door just as the music ended. The club members reached blindly for their drinks as Matsumura dropped besides Andy.

"She is available if you wish it, Midlaa. Actually she rather would like you . . ."

Andy gazed at his peer with glazed eyes. "How do you know?"

"I arranged it," said the fat man, smiling. "She's in room 140, if you're interested of course. All paid for."

"What about you?" Andy protested for politeness' sake.

"Don't worry," said Matsumura. He looked around, then said, "Actually, I've been married for a year now. Don't tell anyone, it would harm my reputation, but I stick to my wife. Go on. For old times' sake."

Room 140 was in semidarkness, lit by a small lamp over the *futon* as Andy slipped inside. The woman was neatly folding the kimono. She wore a light cotton shirt and a suitcase was open in one corner. She looked up as Andy stepped onto the *tatami* mats.

"Ah, . . . The *gaijin*. I was hoping for that. Few foreigners come to this town." She rolled onto her back and spread her legs. "The dancing always makes me hot. Come on now. We can make love later. Just now I need you inside me."

She was hot and sopping wet. Her cunt, large and loose at first, tightened up as Andy rammed into her. Furious with lust he clutched at her narrow muscular behind, his mouth greedily sucking at her nipples. Her fingers dug into his back and she grunted each time he pushed into her. The tattoo she beat on his back fanned his lust, but not enough to cause him to lose complete control. He raised his body slightly to peer into her face. Her eyelids were half shut, only the whites showing, and there was rictus on her lips, her white teeth showing in accompaniment to her eyes.

"Fuck, fuck. Hard. Do it hard," she urged him on, then when the pace of his ramming did not increase, she pulled his head to her roughly. Her lips sought his for a deep penetration of his mouth by her tongue, then a sucking exploration of his mouth while, still under his lips, she muttered encouragement and urgings.

Andy, breathing heavily jerked his hips deep into her slithery welcoming passion. He felt as if his cock was immersed in a liquid bath. Hurriedly, he felt the join between their bodies. Their hair was sopping wet and liquid ran down her thighs and along his balls. She was calling out again, urging him to fuck her, deeper, harder, stronger and her hard blunt fingers pressed into the muscles of his back. Andy raised himself slightly and clutched at her rather flat breasts with both hands.

She gave out a muffled scream. Her hips arched high carrying both of them off the quilt, then she buried her mouth in his shoulder. Andy cried out in pain. Her sharp teeth bit down hard into the muscles of his shoulder bringing blood. He pounded into her as roughly as he could, his cock shuttling deeply into her. She bit again and contracted her muscular dancer's thighs around his bobbing bottom. Andy felt for her ass and squeezed roughly and she bucked again. His hand explored the junction of their bodies again, then he inserted one finger along the pistoning length of his flesh shaft. Another finger was rammed deeply into her clenched asshole. She squealed and bit again and Andy could feel the muscles of her stomach contract against his. Seconds later she was engulfed by a massive series of contractions which milked his cock with unopposable strength.

Andy felt a rush of fluid stream against the fingers between her legs. Then his own orgasm overcame him. Thick gobs of come ran over his questing fingers, mixing with his own liquids, dripping onto the bedding. She clutched at him for one last time, her mouth seeking the bloody marks on his shoulders. Gradually the spasms subsided and Andy collapsed onto her supine body.

They panted heavily together, their mouths touching one another's sweaty skins. She ran her hands over his smooth body, following the hollows where his strong-smelling sweat was collecting. At last the weight of his body on hers became a burden and she rolled him off. Andy lay back on the *futon* and looked at her slim length as she rose. Now that her makeup and the glitter-powder she wore in her hair had come off he could see the faint lines of middle-age on her face. But her body was still slim and muscular, the calves of her legs full, her breasts held proudly erect over a flat stomach. She posed for a second, then turned to head for the bath.

"I must shower," she said, still looking at him. "You will wait?" There was both command and entreaty in her voice. Now that her lust was satisfied, it seemed she was uncertain about him.

"What's your name?" he called after her.

"Utako," she said over her shoulder. It was an odd name, and he pondered differences in naming between town and country as he heard the shower run. He wondered whether to call Jim and tell him where he was, but had forgotten the room number. Instead he rose to a seated position and examined his cock. It was still slick and wet with their juices, and the *futon* was stained with their efforts.

Utako had her back to him when he stepped into the bathroom. Strangely she did not share the normal Japanese passion for baths at any opportunity. Instead the shower head was going full blast. Her face was to the stream and a bar of soap and washcloth were forgotten in her hands. He captured them deftly and maneuvered her out of the full spray while lathering, then rubbing her back briskly with the washcloth. She smiled without opening her eyes. Her back was smooth, marred slightly by two parallel scars which looked to Andy like the remains of some ancient beating. A vicious one. He shuddered in sympathy, dropped the washcloth, and applied his soapy hands to the skin on her buttocks. Obligingly she spread her legs and he soaped her crotch thoroughly, inserting the tip of his soapy fingers between the lips of her cunt. He separated the labiae and soaped her cunt, then inserted the tip of his finger into her puckered anus. She swirled her hips appreciatively until he reluctantly withdrew.

She watched, not offering to help as Andy washed himself, then they rinsed off together in the hot spray. As they dried themselves she questioned him about himself, and proved as adept as he at providing noncommittal answers. Around them they could hear the rowdy sounds of partying visitors.

Dressed in light *yukata* against the mountain cool, they

stroked one another on the *futon*. The door slammed open. A figure in *yukata* staggered into the room. The drunk stared blearily at the two entwined figures. "Scushe me," he hiccupped in surprise. "Wrong room." Still swaying he reached for the door and let himself out. They laughed and her hand reached for his cock again. "Wouldn't he have liked to join us," she said teasingly. His cock sprang erect at her bidding and she rolled over onto her back, her legs spread for their pleasure.

Andy reared back and looked long and hard at her splayed figure. Used to male scrutiny, she bore his examination with patience and humor.

"You like having men stare at you," he said accusingly.

Utako laughed. "In these circumstances, yes. But work? It is just work. It does not matter at all. Don't you like that? Are you jealous?" she asked sweetly. There was a touch of something, malice? concern? fear? in her voice.

Andy smiled. "I like you any way you want. Here, let me prove it to you." His head descended deliberately to her crotch and he kissed the silken damp fur there. She looked on at his brown hair condescendingly. Andy covered her lower lips firmly with his own, then kissed her deeply. His tongue penetrated into her hole, and his lips sucked at hers. The expression on her face changed and she drew a deep ragged breath. Her hands clutched frantically at the *futon* as he set to work, sucking and licking her cunt. His attention wandered from prominent nubbly clitoris to her anus. Careful not to use his teeth, he licked and sucked at every spot he could. His fingers got into the act, drawing her lips apart, allowing his tongue to stimulate every fold of her sweet skin. He clamped his mouth to her lips, ignoring the hairs tickling his nose, and fucked her hole with his tongue, then added a finger, then a second.

At last he raised his head to draw breath. His nose and the lower half of his face were shining with her copious discharge. The *futon* cover on either side of her thighs had been rucked up violently, and the moans that had been muffled by her thighs were only beginning to dwindle. Her eyes were once again half-closed. He saw her face over the nipple-topped hilltops of her breasts. Her breath came raggedly as she pulled him up to her. Her mouth clamped on to his and her arms held him motionless on him for a long while.

"It has never been like this," Utako said. "Men have had me every way there is. It is part of the show. But never like this. Never."

He stroked her face silently. She opened her eyes slowly. There were tears at the corners.

"Some men like putting their mouths on me, down there. But they are demanding their own pleasure. Usually they use their teeth. They like to hear me call out. I even have learned to enjoy the pain. It is a bonus, the pleasure, in addition to what I do. But this is so nice. You are so nice."

"Do you have to sleep with customers?"

"Have to? No. I do it for the bonus, sometimes, or when I see a man I like. I am always horny after several shows in a row, as tonight. . . ." She looked at him in concern. "I am not a whore. I don't sell my body, but . . . public relations . . ." She did not complete the sentence, allowing Andy to guess at the rest. "I have done everything a man and woman can do." she confided. "Really. Everything. Sometimes in public. There is not a part of me that I have not exposed, or used, or had used." Her voice turned hard. "It is a difficult world, and women

must make their way the best they can. I am not
ashamed!'' She said the last fiercely, as if expecting him
to contradict her.

"Nor should you be," he said easily. He kissed her
lightly "I am glad you are experienced.

She laughed, and Andy knew he could hear a sense of
harshness in her tone. But her hand was gentle when she
stroked his back again, then spread her legs. "Come into
me," she whispered.

"Not yet," he whispered cheerfully back.

He rose and knelt between her legs, still smiling. He
ran his palms down from her breasts to her belly, then
down to the valley below. She smiled in anticipation. He
noticed that her cunt was flowing copiously again and his
palms felt slick tracks along her thighs and down to her
knees. Andy pulled at her knees and raised them high,
then brought her feet up as well. Obligingly, she pulled
at her own calves and peered at him from between her
raised knees. He slipped a hard cushion under her head.
The rice husks which made up the bulk of the pillow
rustled soothingly as she moved her head. Their eyes met
as his mouth descended onto her boldly outlined purse.
The lips pouted at the apex of her pubis and he nibbled
them with his lips. She stared at him intently, but as the
sensations became more intense, her eyes began to close.
She breathed irregularly as his mouth, and then his hands,
revisited the core of her womanhood. Gradually, she
began panting in the throes of her lust. Her belly quivered
with suppressed and not-so suppressed sounds. Her blunt
fingers dug valleys into the smooth muscles of her calves.
This time too, Andy did not have to stop so soon. He
varied his movements and their intensity, exploring her
prominently displayed mound. She rocked back and forth
on her back as the first of a series of orgasms overtook

her. He watched the contortions of her face and noted again how the irises of her eyes disappeared, exposing the half-moon whites.

He moved his lips backwards after a series of shakes hit her frame. This time his tongue pecked at the clenched muscles of her ass. She quivered unconsciously, her eyes never opening fully. Her fingers dug even deeper into her calves and the tendons in her legs stood out as the muscles gradually opened to his persistent pressure. This was the first time Andy had ever done this except briefly, but the attraction was so strong he found his sensibilities quietened. And Utako's reactions, the delicate uncontrollable quivering of her body, the extended erection of her nipples, the ridged muscles of her body, and above all, the continuous flow of juices from her liquid cunt were reward enough for his efforts. At last she gave a great cry that seemed to pierce the walls of the room. Her muscles knotted and her head began thrashing wildly on the pillow. "Enough, enough," she managed to mumble brokenly.

Andy wiped his lips on her thighs, then rose to crouch above her. His cock jutted massively out of his fist, like a sword held for action. Her eyes opened slowly and focused on the menacing flesh. Without lowering her legs she reached for him.

"Where do you want it?" he asked. He jabbed the head of his cock lightly at her opened and relaxed anus, then into the sweet smelling slick opening of her cunt.

"Both. Both," Utako said huskily.

Her eyes gradually closed again as Andy sank his cock slowly into the welcoming muscular embrace of her rear hole. The rough tube embraced and milked his shaft for a moment, reluctantly releasing it as he withdrew. Her cunt, softer, wetter, more flaccid, was just as welcoming, just as reluctant to release him. It provided a delightful contrast to the previous entrance. He balanced the contrasts, thrusting into first one, then the other of her holes, his pace quickening and becoming more ragged, as they reached a common climax. In the final moments Andy was no longer conscious which of her holes was receiving him, nor did he know, as he fell asleep, which of her holes was still clutching his softening prick after receiving the full flow of his balls.

# CHAPTER 11:

# SINGER IN THE NIGHT

"This is nice as a vacation, but we really are just screwing around, aren't we?" Jim asked, staring out the window of the bus.

"In more ways than one," Andy said complacently.

"We could go to Mt. Ontake and take vows as mountain priests," Jim continued to grumble. "Let's stop in Takayama, its supposed to be beautiful. In any case, I'm sick of the bus."

Takayama, "The little Kyoto of the mountains," turned out to be a grey and dull city for the most part. The streets were wet with the snow melt and rain. They could not find an inn they liked, and eventually had to settle for a room in one of the new hotels that had sprouted up around the little town.

The hotel was not the quietest of places. Groups of tourists, some foreign, some Japanese, had come up for the cherry blossoms. They wandered around in all stages of dress and undress, calling to one another as the mood took them. A loudspeaker kept on bellowing for members of the Hatosan tour group to do something or other. Maids scurried by with long faces.

"One hell of a place," Jim groused.

"See traditional Japan. The *real* Japan of the samurai and cherry blossoms." Andy laughed grimly. "Hell, even the Japanese haven't seen that. Come on, let's get something to eat."

"But not here. Please, I beg of you, or I'll commit *seppuku* in front of your eyes if I have to eat any of the plastic stuff they probably serve here."

"I'll be your second, then you can do me." Andy consoled Jim. "Maybe we can just march up to the gate of the Clouds people and then they'll shoot us . . ."

The thought sobered both of them. They had had plenty of time to think about what they were doing, and had already considered dropping the whole quest. They stepped into their shoes and headed down the long corridors of the hotel.

There was a band playing in one of the halls just off the lobby. Jim who had enough curiosity for both of them poked his head in through the doorway. He whistled sharply then pulled back. "Hey, Andy, come have a look."

Andy looked in at the source of the sound and abroad smile covered his face. The band was in full swing. The musical quality was noisy, rather than great, but the performers themselves. . . .

"I'll take the drummer," Jim said. She was a slim woman, but her broad shoulders shimmered with sweat in the lights of the hall. Up on stage she was an attraction, her hands moving rapidly across the skins. She wore a short miniskirt, rucked up so that her panties were clearly

visible. Many of the men guests were surreptitiously
enjoying the view. The two guitarists and the singer were
dressed like the drummer in very short gold lame mini-
skirts and tank tops. The lead singer was shaking her long
lustrous black hair and belting out a song about love in
barely recognizable English. They admired the show for
some time, then Andy tugged Jim away.

"I'm hungry, and I'm damned if I'm going to eat in
this plastic palace."

They wandered through the streets, still despondent. By
nightfall, however, the rain had stopped and they had had
a chance to walk around the old quarter of the town.
Wooden buildings, museums, and sense of delicate beauty
washed some of the anxiety from both of them. A hearty
ox-tail soup in a bar near the train station finished the job.

They walked back to the hotel through the wet streets.

"Coffee and some dessert," Andy decided for them.

The hotel coffee shop was surprisingly quiet. They
ordered from a slim sad-waitress. Her Japanese was exe-
crable as was her English. She had a dark face and tiny
nose which went ill with her worried, even frightened
expression. As a waitress she was a disaster, but she
smiled gratefully when Andy managed to catch the sugar
bowl she had almost let slip from her tray. Sugar slid onto
the table. She cast a frightened look over her shoulder at
the manager, a beefy man reading a comic book

"Don't worry," Andy winked at her. "We won't tell."

A party of Japanese came in, then a group of foreign
tourists, twittering about the beauty of the folklore show
they had just seen.

Jim and Andy discussed their plans for the following
day. "Lets just drop it. We'll think of the whole thing as
a holiday and to hell with Clouds and Rain," Andy said.

Jim looked out into the dark. The garden was almost

invisible. This late the floodlights had been switched off. The party of foreign tourists talked loudly and volubly at a nearby table.

"Yeah, I guess we'd better. I've got a bad feeling about all of this. Maybe we should talk to Michiko Teraoka? Maybe she can give us some advice."

"Look she's only a lowly traffic cop, and a woman to boot . . ."

"Yeah, but maybe she knows someone higher up, and in any case, would know whether we ought to go to the police at all. I mean, after all, we only have some vague threats to go on, nothing concrete . . ." He was interrupted by a resounding crash. One of the tourists stood up and swore in English. He was large beefy man, his face red. His pants were stained with coffee. The diminutive waitress stood before him dumbly, her tray in her hands. The manager raced towards the ruckus.

"Stupid bitch!" The tourist glared at the girl and swore again in a heavy Australian accent. "Clumsy bloody wog. My best pair of pants, too."

The manager tried to calm the tourist down, in broken English, while threatening death and destruction to the girl in Japanese. She hid her face and her shoulders were trembling.

The tourist was still ranting on and the manager looked about him helpless at the anger and rudeness of the guest's attack. He tried apologizing again in broken English and received in return threats of law suits and complaints that went quite over his head. Jim and Andy looked at one another then rose and joined the altercation.

"Excuse me," Andy said in English. The tourist sputtered to a stop. "The manager just wanted to apologize. He says the girl is new . . ."

"Hey, you speak English. Thought you were a Jap."

"It really wasn't her fault, Jack," one of the others in the party said. "If ye hadn't moved about so much, ye wouldn't have made her drop the tray."

The beefy man considered the fact for a moment while Andy rapidly soothed the manager in perfect Japanese.

Faced with someone who could speak intelligibly and was obviously able to calm the situation, the manager returned to his normal polite public face. He bowed smoothly and stopped abusing the girl.

"Tell the guest I am sorry. The girl is not a regular waitress. I will have his suit cleaned. . . ."

Jim translated and together they managed to placate both parties. All this time the waitress stood there, her hands clasped before her thighs, her eyes downcast. The manager brusquely ordered her to bring drinks *carefully* for the tourist party, and Jim and Andy returned to their seats.

"I am very grateful to you," the manager approached them quietly. The waitress hovered quietly in the background. "She is so stupid and untrained."

"Don't be too hard on her," Jim requested in the polite mode. "I am sure it was not her fault. One of the tourists as much as said that."

"Nonetheless, . . ." the manager cast a baleful eye at the girl. "Are you staying at the hotel?" he asked politely.

"Yes." Jim pointed out the keyholder with its large numeral.

"Then enjoy your stay," he bowed deeply and walked off.

The *futon* had been laid out side by side in the middle of the room. Jim stretched hugely and wondered whether to have a bath. Andy simply dropped his clothes in a heap, snapped open the starched *nemaki* robe the hotel provided instead of pyjamas, and flopped onto the bedding.

There was a knock on the door. They looked at one

another in sudden panic. They knew no one here and proximity to the Clouds and Rain headquarters made them both
nervous. Jim swallowed and Andy said "Enter!" nervously. Both stood on the *tatami,* the tension in their legs
palpable.

"*Gomen kudasai,*" the coffee-shop manager stood
there. The waitress hovered behind them.

Jim and Andy looked at the man in perplexity. "Please,
come in," they said in unison. The man and woman
stepped through the door. The nightingale floor at the
entrance which served as an intruder alarm squeaked musi-
cally as the manager crossed it. He did not step into the
room itself, merely shoving the waitress in ahead of him.
She had taken off her apron and wore only the simple
mother-hubbard she had worked in.

Th manager bowed. "I am very grateful to you gentlemen for what you did. Please accept my apologies for any
inconvenience."

They both denied any such thing, but the manager continued. "I thought I could make up to you for the unpleas-
antness. I will leave her with you. I'm sure you can make
use of her." He bowed again and both Jim and Andy's
jaws dropped open. They stared for a minute at the girl,
then back at the manager.

"She is yours if you want her," the cafe owner said,
roughly shoving the girl into the room. "I assure you, she
is no trouble. Normally I charge, of course, but since you
were so kind . . . In any case, there have been no requests
for her tonight. Very obedient," he added with a grin.

"Obedient?" Andy asked, puzzled at the emphasis.

The cafe owner nodded. "Yes, today Japanese women
are not as they used to be," he sighed, apparently in
memory of the good old days. "Now they demand too
much, offer too little. This one, on the other hand. Any-

thing, anything at all. The older men go for that very much of course. The younger ones, eh, sahh, they don't know what it is all about now, do they?'' He smiled, bowed politely and left. The nightingale floor at the entrance to the room sang his departure.

"You're obedient?'' Andy asked thoughtfully, examining the slight form as the girl stepped towards them.

Jim looked on curiously.

"I am Krish,'' said the girl nervously. Her Japanese was poor and she had a strong accent.

Andy just looked on. He simply had no idea what to do with her.

"Take off your clothes,'' Jim ordered uncertainly. He was unused to "obedient,'' and the taste was strange to his ears, but he was interested in finding out precisely what the word meant in this context.

She raised her hand to the shoulder of her dress and slid the print sack-like garment over her head. Underneath she wore nothing but string panties, the pink front barely covering the tiny patch of night-black hair at the junction of her legs. The panties slipped down as the two men watched, hypnotized partly by her femaleness, partly by the sensation of power she created in them, and by fear of that sensation.

"Come here and lie down,'' Jim said hoarsely.

She obeyed without any visible emotion showing on her face.

Andy laid a hand on the curve of her thigh and could feel the trembling under her skin. She looked back at him, her dark almond eyes fathomless. He remembered the coffee shop owner's words "Very obedient,'' and for a moment, ashamed of himself, he wondered at what price to her that obedience had been instilled. But the warmth of her presence and the urgency of his own needs

restrained any noble gesture on his part. And behind her
he could see Jim's hand moving on her back in gentle
stroking motions. He could see in Jim's eyes that he felt
it, too.

Andy began rubbing her warm brown skin. Her breasts
were tiny firm hills tipped by chocolate nipples. Though
her hips were wide for her build, her mons was tiny,
capped by a feathery growth of coal black hair. He ran
his hands gently over her skin, stroking her breasts and
belly, touching her thighs with the tips of his fingers.

Jim felt her respond to Andy's motions and he allowed
himself the luxury of some exploration. He squeezed the
full balls of her ass gently and she trembled at his touch.
Her neck and back muscles were rigid and he could feel
the beat of her pulse as he stroked her neck. She lay there
tinily between the two of them, completely obedient to
their wants. He bit his lip thoughtfully for a moment then
said, "Lie on your stomach."

Krish rolled over obediently, though there was a percep-
tible quiver in the muscles of her back. Andy looked at
his brother in surprise. It was usually his own particular
preference, not Jim's, and he was disappointed that his
twin had not gotten the same sense of helplessness from
the girl.

To Andy's surprise Jim did not mount the girl. Instead
he began massaging her, working away at the tense muscles of her neck and back. After a while the dark fathomless eyes closed and the tension started very slowly to
dissipate. Andy joined in Jim's work. He was the better
masseur of the two, tracing her delicate muscles beneath
the smooth skin, rubbing them firmly but gently, avoiding
putting any pressure on her bones. Gradually the tension
began leaving her. They spread her legs apart and she
tensed slightly, relaxing again as each of the men took

one of her calves and kneaded it carefully. They repeated the motions with her feet, and she giggled silently at the touch of *farang* hands on her nether extremities.

Loosely relaxed as a rag doll she allowed them to roll her over on her back and kneed the muscles in her arms and chest. She looked and noted with surprise that neither of them were erect. They ignored her inspection, intent on their self-imposed task.

Slowly, so as not to disturb the wonderful feeling of their hands as they worked at her, she took each dangling male member in a soft hand. She tugged at the male extensions slowly and gently, noting with pleasure how they thickened in her fists without actually rising in protest with the treatment. The two cocks, one slightly paler than the other rose to full erection and the two men looked down at her, not demanding, merely questioning. She raised her knees until they touched the tips of her breasts, then led the paler of the two cocks to the delicate petal-lips of her cunt. The paler *farang* looked down at her cunt. She appreciated the compliment and waited for him to see his fill, then slipped the tip of his cock between her lips. He adjusted his body and she smiled her gratitude for the fact that he squatted before her rather than precipitating his entire weight onto her body. She pulled him forward into her with one hand while playing with Jim's erect cock with the other. Guiding his movements she made sure his pace was adjusted to her own pleasure. Gradually her dark-lashed eyes closed and she felt the movement of his hips against her curled body as her feet supported him and her tiny cunt brought him to a shivering climax.

Her channel was full and juicy now, and she wondered whether to clean herself, but the other *farang* was impatiently waiting for his turn, and her own demands were starting to rise. Jim squatted before the girl's parted knees and guided his erect cock into the overflowing opening. She urged him on with touches of her knees against his flanks. Carefully, so as not to impose his weight on her, he jabbed his cock in corkscrewing motions into her narrow opening. She matched his movements perfectly. His balls began to clench in preparation for the eruption to come and he hastily seized control of his thoughts. Mechanically almost he stroked her body. Andy joined in, then leaned forward and sucked on each of her tiny nipples alternatively. Krisha smiled at Jim over his brother's brown hairs and dug one of her long-nailed hands into his ass while stroking the wavy brown hair that lay on her breast.

Digging his hands under her slim buttocks, Jim set to work in earnest to please the small Thai girl. He ground his hips at hers, then alternated that with deep and shallow thrusts. She smiled faintly, her eyes narrowing. As her climax approached she began breathing in tight little puffs of air. The breaths grew quicker and shallower as Andy found her tiny clitoris with his fingers and as Jim raised her buttocks, forcing them to meet his own thrusts. She cried out something in Thai and both her hands beat at Andy's shoulders then subsided as her climax ebbed. Finally she opened her eyes to look at the two *farang*.

Andy lay, his head pillowed on her tiny breast from one side. Jim stopped puffing and crawled to the other. Together the three of them lay in a huddle, warming one another with the touch of their skins. She explored the two male bodies idly with her hands. An idea occurred to her and she pushed the two men off, reached for her dress. She ignored the tiny pink panties and the matching hair band.

"You're going?" Jim asked, half in question. At the back of his mind was the knowledge that he could order her to stay. "Very obedient."

"You very nice," she said in her broken Japanese. "Good man. Good feel."

Andy smiled lazily at the compliment. He wanted to reach for her again, but the idea of forcing himself upon her was now repellent. She had taken the edge of his lust and he felt no urgency. Her next words surprised both the men.

"I bring my friends," Krisha said in a bright voice.

"Friends?" they asked.

She giggled, pulled the sacklike dress over her head and slipped out of the room. In a few minutes there were rustlings and twitterings at the door of the room and they were invaded by Krisha and three more figures. Jim suddenly recognized them. Two still wore the glittery miniskirted pinafores. They were the members of the all girl band.

Jim and Andy rose naked and bowed. There was little else they could do. The four brown faces giggled and one covered her face at the sight of the two male crotches, then ogled the cocks again.

Not knowing what to do, Jim fell back on the regularities of hospitality. They were soon all sitting in a circle, plates of snacks scattered between them. Two of the girls drank beer, the other two tea. Krisha appeared to be the only one with even a smattering of Japanese. One of the others, Sattisanoya, could speak some English. The other two not at all.

"Hot," Krisha said succinctly. She rose and slipped out of her dress. The other three did the same, displaying their femininity to the two men without the slightest hesitation. None of them had on any underclothes. All had the same slim build. Sattaya held up her breasts which were larger than those of the others and said something in Thai.

"You like?" Krisha asked.

Jim nodded. Andy tried to be bolder and pointed to his semierect cock. The girls blushed and giggled and Andy's face took on an expression of bewilderment.

"Not nice point. Not nice point people," Krisha said, her face contorted in merriment. She turned her face away and pointed to his erect cock. The other girls giggled and hid their faces, too.

"Then we should hide it," Jim said suddenly. "This one, too . . ." He pantomimed covering his now erect cock with the palm of his hand. Krisha smiled and nodded her approval, then said something in her own language.

"We make show for you?" Sattisanoya asked coquettishly.

Wordlessly the two men nodded their agreement. The girls reached for one another. They were soon entwined in a tangle of brown limbs and bodies that formed an erotic arabesque. Lips against cunts, legs entwined with arms. They displayed the most amazing flexibility Jim or Andy had ever seen. Their bronze limbs slid over one another. At one point Sattaya was peering at Andy from between Pensri's legs while Krisha was rubbing her own fur with her foot. Her leg was wrapped around someone else's thigh.

Andy stood up suddenly. His eyes were glowing and inarticulate noises came from his mouth. He hurled himself into the pile of naked limbs. His cock stabbed desperately at the soft brown skin before him. Magically, it seemed, a path opened before him. Sattisanoya's face appeared at the level of his belly, peering at him from over her feet that seemed folded in her lap. The pink slit of her cunt was fully exposed, framed by scant black hairs and by the warm bronze of her thighs. Andy lunged forward and his cock sank deeply into a slick resistant channel. He groped for her mouth with his. Someone else suddenly obscured her face and he found his tongue slipping into a tight warm cunt. The taste and smell intoxicated him and he thrust away at both tight channels, barely conscious that Jim was somewhere in the pile as well.

His cock was suddenly in the open air and he sought desperately for the warm comforting flesh. It was captured by a warm mobile hole, and by the sharp touch of teeth, he knew that one of the girls had captured it in her mouth. The sensation was confirmed as the mouth began sucking strongly at his cock. Another mouth clamped over his balls. He was about to explode when a firm small hand squeezed the base of his cock ruthlessly. A tiny voice whispered "Sorry," and the mouth was replaced by another soft pussy.

Jim watched the tangle for only a short moment before he too was sucked under. A slim hand emerged from the pile and pulled him in. He found himself enmeshed in a pit of frenzied skin that absorbed his cock, his tongue, the fingers of all hands and his toes. He wished he had had some more pricks, sure that they would have been accommodated in the scrum.

It was a long time before the four Thai girls allowed the two *farang* to empty themselves. One of them had his cock between Sattaya's breasts when she felt him beginning to pulse. She called out for the others to watch and they were rewarded by spurt after spurt of creamy fluid. Her breasts were smeared with the stuff. She smelt it delicately, and made a face. "Just like any other male," she said wonderingly."

"What did you expect? Coconut milk?" someone teased.

Pensri was on her hands and knees, her feet tucked well under her. One of the *farang* was heaving away over her and she was smiling slightly. She felt the start of his contractions and one of her friends lowered her mouth between the two bodies and licked furiously at the frothing shaft. The man erupted with a groan, his hands busy with parts of the other girls.

Gradually the action slowed down. At last they lay together. One of the girls prepared tea, which they all sipped gratefully. The girls rose and pulled on their dresses.

"You come Pattaya, in Thailand, you ask for Golden Girls," Krisha said by way of parting. The two men nodded and bowed.

# CHAPTER 12:

# NIGHT RIDERS

The morning was dull and grey. They looked at train schedules. They could return to Tokyo via Nagoya or via the coast. Either way was long, and the way back in the direction of Nagoya boring, as they had already done it twice during the week.

"How about a bus to Matsumoto, then a train to Ueno? That would be different."

Jim shrugged irritably. He was sleepy, worried about their failed attempt to reach the Clouds and Rain people and find out why they were being hounded, and annoyed at the weather.

They walked gloomily to the bus depot. At that hour of the morning the buses did not seem too attractive. The depot was gloomy and the passengers seemed composed of people with stomach aches or chronic illness or both.

There were two couples, obviously honeymooners buying tickets for Matsumoto, too. They all wandered off to the bay where the bus was to arrive.

It was one of the newer tour buses, equipped with a

small refrigerator for drinks and even a toilet in the back, like the large American Greyhounds. It backed into its bay, directed by the shrill whistles of the bus guide. Apparently, sleepy as they had been, they had bought tickets for the scenic route. Jim groaned inwardly. The last thing he needed was a jolly guided tour, complete with clicking cameras and cheery guide holding a flag to lead her flock along.

Andy looked on appreciatively as the guide backed the bus into position with blasts from her whistle. She wore a prussian-blue uniform with matching pillbox hat. Her calves were rather thick, but she had a pert face under the hat, and an imposing bosom buttoned into the uniform jacket.

They boarded, grey faced. Only Andy somewhat more cheerful as he winked at the guide. She smiled back mechanically.

The rest of the passengers were a mixed bag. The two newlywed couples, the wives twittering and fussing over their new possessions, the possessions in question trying to appear as if they were not new to the whole thing. Two middle-aged women. Two middle-aged men. Another couple.

As the bus was about to leave two figures dashed to the door, hammering on it desperately. One was a blonde woman, obviously American. She hastily seated herself nervously on the front seat, near the driver. She wore a heavy skirt and flat sensible shoes. She was rather mousy and nondescript but for the long blond hair. The other passenger was a roly-poly man in dark glasses. He talked hurriedly to the driver, dropped his belongings, picked them up again after apologizing, apologized again and backed off the bus.

"All that fuss to find out he was in the wrong bus?" Jim laughed.

"Hairy legs," Andy said judiciously.

"What?" Jim peered at his brother. "How do you know? He was wearing pants."

"Not him. Her. The missionary. I was trying to decide if she was good enough for me. She has hairy legs."

"How do you know she's a missionary?"

"That kind *always* are missionaries."

"Nonsense."

They debated the missionary question all the way out of town, as the Kiso mountains rose above them. Andy was all for burning them at the stake. Jim preferred them pickled, in fiery *shochu* liquor preferably. "That way they can't preach, but might still be of some use."

"As what?"

"Door stops. Waiters. I don't know. There's some good in everyone."

"Well, maybe. But for your sanity I'd suggest you stay away from her."

The day was not as dreary as Jim had feared it would be. They visited some of the places along the route, but because of the cloudy weather, stops were kept at a minimum. Even the intrepid Japanese tourists preferred to huddle in the warmth of the bus rather than brave the snow flurries. Since the bus was half empty, everyone had plenty of room. Seat backs were made to recline, and the guide distributed food and drink freely. When she bent over him, Andy made a point of peering down her white blouse at the expanse of breast that nestled inside. She kept her professional calm, but Andy noticed her color deepened every time she looked at him.

The weather got progressively worse. Snow, one of the late falls of spring, battered at the bus windows. The bus slowed to a crawl. The driver conferred with the guide and they worriedly examined the road signs, wondering whether to turn back. They appeared to be the only ones on the mountain road. The driver muttered to himself. He was a young man with strong hands and an intent expression, but the rigors of driving in what had turned into a major snowstorm were making his hands quiver. The blonde looked out the windshield, then at the driver, worry plain on her face. He tried to flash her a reassuring smile. She smiled tentatively back.

The way turned pitch black and Jim realized they were in a tunnel. The driver stopped the bus abruptly. He peered ahead, then slowly eased the bus forward. The passengers fell silent. The driver stopped the bus suddenly, muttered something under his breath then opened the door and hurried out of the bus. Passengers craned their necks to see what the problem was. The driver returned, shivering. He took the microphone.

"I apologize for the delay. It seems there has been a snowslide. This side of the tunnel is blocked. We cannot continue. I will try to back up and then turn around and return to Takayama. I am sorry for the inconvenience."

The guide dropped from the bus and directed the reverse with her whistle. They backed up the long tunnel. Suddenly the whistle shrilled for a stop. The guide appeared again. Her face was white. "The tunnel is blocked on the other side, too!" she called. All the passengers could hear her without the use of the loudspeaker. The driver slumped at the wheel. The passengers jabbered at one another, their voices rising to a crescendo.

"Don't worry. Don't worry please," the driver entreated them, using the microphone again. "There is no danger. There is plenty of air, we have food and tea. The bus will be warm. The highway people will come with snow plows to get us out soon. They know we are due in Matsumoto.''

"Not till late in the evening,'' one of the passengers said.

"Please don't panic,'' the guide found her voice.

The blonde passenger in the front seat started to scream.

Bedlam ensued. The guide calmed the blonde woman first, then worked her way down the aisle, soothing the passengers. She left the blonde in care of the driver. He patted her shoulder and offered her tea and her panicked crying turned to sobs. She laid her head on his shoulder and he comforted her, his face bearing an embarrassed look that soon turned thoughtful.

Andy watched the approach of the guide with the tea. He felt strange. His pulse was hammering in his temples and he was suddenly conscious of a massive erection. His eyes were stuck to her form as if hypnotized. The two male passengers who had been drinking from small whiskey bottles in a forward seat watched her, too. Her hips had acquired a seductive rolling motion as she moved and unconsciously she smoothed her skirt down her thighs. She handed Andy his tea, then turned to Jim who was sitting across the aisle. As delicately as he could Andy ran his hands up her leg, touching her stockings lightly with the back of his hand. She gave no sign of having noticed, merely moving on to the two women behind Jim.

She reached the back seats of the bus. The two honeymoon couples had ensconced themselves there. One of the men looked up at her approach with dazed eyes, then turned back to the woman next to him. She was a plump bespectacled girl. Her shirt was open and her breasts were being mauled by the man's hands. Her hands were fumbling inexpertly at his crotch where an obvious bulge was growing.

The other couple was similarly engaged, the woman straddling the man, her skirt hiked up, her panties hanging from one bare foot. The guide looked on for a moment. Then she turned slowly, as if dazed and reluctant to leave, and retraced her steps to the front of the bus.

"May I have some more tea, please?" She automatically stopped to respond to the request. It was the young *gaijin* who had been staring at her. She bent over to hand him the plastic bottle of hot green tea.

He stared into her eyes for a brief moment, and when her eyes dropped away, he followed the line of her neck to the smooth bulge of her full breasts. His hands rose quickly and shovelled themselves into her blouse, squeezing at the rubbery-tipped mounds and pulling her to him. She struggled silently for a moment, then fell down on top of him. Involuntarily his hips jerked up against the softness of her bosom. She panted heavily, giving no thought to her voice. He pulled her to him. A shadow fell over them. Two shadows to be exact. The men who had been drinking and talking throughout the ride were peering down at the struggling couple intently.

For a second they just stood there. Andy pulled at the seat button and reclined the back as far as it would go. As if the maneuver had been rehearsed, the other two gripped the guide gently but irresistibly. Andy looked aside, intent on inviting Jim to join them from across the aisle, but saw that Jim was involved with his own affairs.

One of the two middle-aged women sitting behind Jim leaned forward over his shoulder as they sat and waited. He tried to ignore her and concentrate on quieting the bulge in his pants. He watched the driver and the foreign girl. They were huddled together on the bus bench, and there was a sense of rapid and furtive movement. The two women behind him whispered to one another for a brief instant, then one of them rose and slid into the seat beside Jim. She had a round face and her short black hair framed it well, making it appear plumper than it really was. She smoothed down the creases of her grey skirt, smiled at him showing somewhat crooked teeth behind full red-painted lips and asked, "Are you Japanese?"

"No," he said briefly, not wishing to be rude, but disturbed unreasonably by her proximity.

"This is terrible," she said in a friendly manner. "The bus company should not allow this to happen. I am ashamed for them."

"Yes," chimed in the other one, behind them. "They will have to compensate us heavily!"

Jim turned to her. She had long hair in a thick braid wound around her head. Her face was slightly pock-marked, but rather long, her mouth wide. Both her beringed hands were resting on the back of his seat, near his neck. He could see the pulsing in the delicate blue veins under the smoothness of her skin: strong and erratic. His own heart beat in response. He turned for some help to Andy. His brother was rapt in some private fantasy. Jim followed his brother's gaze for an instant. Andy's neck was twisted around as he followed the movements of the guide down the aisle. His eyes were glazed and fixed on the blue uniform.

"You like girls?" the woman next to Jim asked conspiratorially.

Considering the condition of his prick, Jim thought the question superfluous. The Japanese had a genius for asking the obvious. "Yes, I do," he answered shortly.

Her eyes dropped for an instant to the bulge in his jeans and then she raised wide innocent-looking eyes to him. There was a strange spark in them Jim was not sure he recognized. "I am Komatsuzaki Fumiko and this is my friend Hotate Tsuya. We are from Hiroshima. You know Hiroshima?"

"No, I've never been there," Jim said. "What are you doing here? I mean is this your vacation?"

"Oh no, Tsuya-chan and I have just been at a sales meeting. We work for a large *depaato* in Hiroshima. This is only a day off for recreation. We are very glad you are here with us." She licked her red lips, her eyes drawn inexorably to Jim's crotch.

"Enough of this foolishness," Tsuya's voice came at them from the gloom. She stood up behind Jim and leaned forward. Her ample bosom, encased in a loose sweater descended onto the crown of his head just as her hands grasped his cheeks and tilted his face up to hers. For a brief moment he was conscious of the strangeness of her face peering down upside down to his, and then her mouth descended and fastened leech-like onto his own. His first reaction was to grab at her hands and try to pull them away, but she was stronger than she looked and in any case, he was in a bad position. By then the sensation of her probing tongue had reached his hindbrain and his hands, completely without any volition on his part, pulled the mound of her hair to him. They kissed frenziedly. She ground her lips and teeth at him, moaning and growling in her throat. Then her hands left his cheeks and started unbuttoning his shirt just as he felt Fumiko's hands fumbling at his fly. What the hell, he said to himself, and spared one hand for Fumiko. Her breasts were enclosed in a thick blouse and no less thick bra.

Fumiko bestrode him, her full cunt squishing down onto his erection. Jim felt powerful and alert. He urged Tsuya around, out of her seat and onto the one he shared with Fumiko. His mouth was busy with the breast Fumiko held up to him, while one hand was engaged with the softer, rounder breast presented to him by her friend. His right hand was in his crotch, pinching roughly at Fumiko's rapidly moving clitoris. She whispered into his ear, nibbling gently then harder as her passion rose. His mouth shuttled between the four breasts presented to him, and his kisses were liberally mixed with nips from his teeth. Both he and the two women were breathing heavily. Fumiko bounced over him with abandon, her heavy frame descending and mashing him to the seat unmercifully. Then she changed her pace and began a grinding motion on his lap. He clutched at her generous hips. His loins pushed up at her with main strength and she shrieked as she felt the first of his orgasm pulsing into her depths. She urged him on, her own climax only seconds behind, clutching at his head and pulled him to her.

They rested thus for a few seconds, and the Tsuya's harsh voice cut into their relaxed haze. "Now me," she said, and the plump Fumiko relinquished her seat. She rose slowly and reluctantly off the still erect shaft. Tsuya regarded it blandly for a moment. "I am glad you haven't exhausted him," was her dry comment. She fisted the shaft with a few brisk motions, then straddled the waiting man. For a start she pumped up and down on him, offering him her full rather soft and sagging breasts. Then as they both started taking an interest in things, she rose suddenly and turned around.

Jim got one full glimpse of her bottom and then she had captured his cock again. She bent forward and Jim found the position much more comfortable. She grasped his hands and brought them to her breasts. Her nipples were prominent and the full fleshy bags soft to the touch. She forced his fingers deep into the yielding masses. Jim took the hint and started mashing her breasts firmly. She grunted in delight and started bouncing on him rapidly while addressing Fumiko with her hands. Jim saw Fumiko sink to the floor of the bus in the gloom, then his hips twitched in surprise as he felt her tongue lapping at the join of his and Tsuya's crotches.

He leaned over Tsuya. The braid was becoming undone and obscured his vision, but he could see her strong capable hands holding Fumiko's face to her crotch. The sensation of Fumiko's knowledgeable tongue urged him forward into dark clouds of lust and he pulled the woman to him with a lustful abandon that brought a shriek of pleasure from her lips. From the front of the bus he could hear the loud squeals of the hysterical blonde. Vaguely he wondered whether he should go to her aid.

In the front seat Millicent Purdue was recalling the words often spoken at Bible House in Dubuque. When in trouble, pray to the Lord and remember, love conquers all. What she was feeling at the moment was not precisely what her teachers at the missionary seminar had intended by the word love. It was more akin to what she had felt for her departed husband. The smell of the young bus driver was driving her mad, and she recalled, not without guilt, how she would sniff unobtrusively at Donald's shirts as she put them into the wash. The driver was sitting close to her, patting and stroking her head and speaking slowly in Japanese. She could barely understand the words, but she found herself wanting to respond to his actions with some of her own. She glanced down at her own hand and discovered to her horrified surprise that she was indeed stroking his trouser leg, very close to a suspicious and large bulge in his pants.

She pulled back from his embrace. "We must get down on our knees and pray to God."

The young driver, perhaps misunderstanding her on purpose said, "The *kami* have nothing to do with it. The

highway department does. Are you cold?" He watched
her shivering with concern, then stripped of his jacket and
laid it across her shoulders. His own, she noticed, were
broad and heavy. Her shivering was not from fear, but
from the sudden wave of an emotion she could not pin-
point. She hid her face and found herself staring directly
at the bulge in his serge pants. Her hand trembled and she
tried to fight an irresistible urge to touch the mound.

"What is your name?" she managed to croak out. They
both watched fascinated as her pale long-fingered hand
trembled towards his crotch.

"Yanagisato Kaoru," he said in a whisper. The bulge
in his pants grew the closer her hand got. His hand was
still automatically stroking her blonde hair, though now
she was conscious of the fact that he was stroking much
deeper into the blonde mass.

She let out a broken sob which seemed to be echoed
from the back of the bus. Her hand sought and found the
object of her desire, and she clutched at a stiff rod hidden
by cloth. The sensation brought back memories of feeling
for Donald in the dark, before he had been caught dead
with that floozy, and she suddenly realized that for all she
had been married for two years, she had never seen a
man's member. She unzipped his pants and his hands
poised on her hair. The heart shaped tip, deep brownish-
pink in color stared back at her out of a single eye. She
traced the peculiar shape with the tips of her fingers.
Beneath the broad hoodlike shelf she found soft loose skin
wrapped around a warm stiff shaft. Moved by impulse she
moved the skin up and down. The entire shaft quivered
in response. She held the shaft tightly in her fist, then in
a quick birdlike motion bent forward and kissed the tip.
She was shocked by her own temerity. She had never, in
all her life, even heard of such a thing. Trying to withdraw

she found her head held down, gently but firmly. For the period of a heartbeat she considered, then with a wordless sigh of longing fulfilled, she opened her mouth and engulfed the thick pole. At first she merely allowed the head between her lips, exploring it with her tongue. But quite soon the spirit of exploration overcame her and she moved it deeper into her mouth. She was conscious that Kaoru's hands had left her head and she was free to go. She used this movement not to retreat, but to move her head up and down his shaft. She felt his hands on the front of her blouse, opening it, and then pushing down the bra underneath. The feel of his large capable hands on her breasts was almost more than she could bear. Another hunger started growing in her loins and she wished to feel his hands between her legs as well. She became bolder in her explorations. She hollowed her cheeks and sucked tentatively at the shaft. The rewards were immediate. Kaoru's frame stiffened and pushed more of his shaft into her. His hands strummed at her flat nipples, twiddling them in a frenzy. Millicent set to work with a will, bobbing her head up and down the shaft while sucking at it as well as she could.

One of Kaoru's hands left her breast to her disappointment. She was consoled as it slid up her folded bare leg in search of her crotch. He twitched aside the cotton panties and rested on her full bush, then sought the wet lips of her cunt. Only Donald's fingers had been there before, and she admitted to herself that she missed the infrequent touches even in those long ago days. She wondered whether Donald had ever had one of the women he was with do this to him. At the thought she sucked harder as the driver's broad fingers penetrated her vagina. For a brief second she wondered, this time in fright, what would happen if the guide would return and see them as they were now, and then the pleasure of the act banished all thoughts from her head.

The three men stretched the guide against the back of the seat. Holding her down with his thighs and weight, Andy rapidly undid the buttons of her uniform jacket. Her breasts rose and fell in agitation. Around them they could hear the sounds of sex in the long vehicle. The guide's eyes were closed as she struggled. Moans escaped from the imprisoned mouth. Andy unbuttoned the white blouse beneath her jacket. Under it a white slip hid her breasts. He wondered whether to tear it, then found that there were minute buckles on the straps which allowed him to loosen the garment. Her breasts were encased in frothy lace, joined in front by a clasp. She gazed at him wide eyed as he undid the clasp and the two cups that had held her breasts imprisoned sprang apart. Her breasts were full, stretched mounds over her ribcage. He hungrily sucked on each erect nipple for a second. His assistants licked their lips. Andy fumbled underneath the prone girl and rapidly stripped her blue-grey skirt off. The slip followed. Her panties, bedecked with tiny pink flowers hid her mound completely. He pulled them and the pantyhose off. At last she was magnificently naked. Her golden brown form was exposed to his eyes. She started struggling again as he parted her thighs. Without avail. Her uncomfortable position gave her few options, and within a second he was lying between her legs. His cock felt like an iron bar. He positioned it with difficulty at the slick entrance to her cunt. The sexual excitement had encompassed her, too, notwithstanding her initial reluctance, and the entrance was sopping with her internal liquids.

Andy shoved forward and the head of his cock penetrated her waiting vagina. She gave a piercing shriek, which was answered hungrily by other people in the carriage.

Andy was unable to give any thought to her pleasure. He was overcome with his own lust and his cock shuttled in and out of her without pause or variation. They were both calling out incoherently as their mutual orgasm overcame them. She clutched at Andy and her insides rippled milking him of the last of his juices. He found he was still erect and she looked over his head as his cock continued hammering at her soft insides. She gurgled something incomprehensible and he hummed into the nipple on her firm breast. Other hands were searching at her body and she moved slightly to accommodate them. She trembled again as she came violently, shaking his hips roughly with her hands. Andy's response was a spurt of pleasure as he climaxed, too, grinding his hips into her shaking loins for the second time. He was urged off the guide's spread body by one of his assistants. The man, in late middle age, buried himself immediately between her thighs. He grunted and rooted about, and she bore his thrusting coolly, then suddenly went into a paroxysm of movement. The man stiffened in her arms, raised his torso to stare blindly at her face, then collapsed. Only the heaving and pulsing of his bottom told of the spray of viscous fluid erupting from his balls and spraying her interior. He was pulled off her by his friend who was as hurried as his immediate predecessor. This time the guide locked her legs around his back, urging him on with dovelike cooes. Andy slid a hand between the two heaving bodies and pinched her luxurious breasts, she peered up at him gratefully and squeezed her interior muscles as best she could. As she felt the first pulses of the man's rising orgasm, she felt herself explode for the fourth time. The heavy weight of her third lover of the night slid off her. The two older men tottered off to their seats. The *gaijin* leaned over her. He dipped his head and kissed her deeply, then slid into the seat beside her. For a moment she regretted he did not climb on top of her immediately, then realized that her muscles were cramped.

"What is your name?" Andy asked, cradling her head gently against his chest.

"Someya Hana," she whispered. She started trying to cover her nakedness with her hand, then desisted as Andy squeezed her large breast.

"Are you cold?" he asked solicitously.

"No," she said. "Not as long as you hold me. I wonder if they will be looking for us?" she asked inconsequentially.

"Then they shouldn't find us too soon. I would like to love you again," Andy said. His fingers played with her nipple, which sprang erect. Hana turned her face to his chest and nuzzled at the springy surface. "My name is Andy."

"*Hajimemashite,*" she said, then giggled at the formality. "I would like that very much," she whispered. "I enjoyed you the most of all the men."

"And the others?"

She shuddered briefly and licked his chest hungrily. "I was frightened at first. But the desire was so . . . so overpowering. I liked them, too. I have never been like that, but I needed you all." Her licks turned to demanding nibbles as she sucked lightly at his chest. "And now I need you again."

"Not yet," Andy laughed. "Give me a minute or two . . ."

"Maybe I should go and find out if the driver has sighted the rescue party," she wondered aloud. Andy stopped her lips with his own. He hoped the rescue would not arrive too soon. There were still many things to be done. His hand squeezed her breast again.

Kaoru pulled his three fingers out of Millicent's cunt and pushed her head back. She stared at him in understanding. He sniffed at his fingers, enjoying her aroma then rose from her. For a second he cast a look back along the bus, then smiled. Millicent raised her head to look in the same direction. In the gloom of the bus's emergency lights she could see several groups of figures all moving together on the seats. Three men were piled together with a woman she recognized as the young guide in one of the seats. The feet of another woman were projecting into the aisle and another one was bent forward over the same seat. Far in the back there were other movements, sighs, moans both female and male. She turned back to the driver with shining eyes. He dropped his pants and displayed his cock and balls growing out of a mass of black hairs. He pushed her firmly backwards and she rested comfortably on her pack, her lips moist with anticipation.

Kaoru flipped up the fair-skinned missionary's plain skirt and she aided him by raising her hips. He pulled at the plain cotton underwear. It was damp at the crotch and he slid it easily down her legs. She had a lush bush of blonde hair running from between her legs almost up to her belly button and spreading to either side in a wide triangle. For a moment he contemplated the sight in the dim light. Then he raised her right leg over the headrest on the seat. Millicent watched his face, first with concern, afraid he would think her ugly *there* then with growing joy as she recognized his pleasure at the sight.

Kaoru noticed the full growth of hair. The hairy curls extended well back to her anus. He knew it to be perverse of him, but he preferred fully haired women to smooth ones. He licked his lips, wondering whether to tongue her first. He would have liked to eat her to a climax, but his own needs were urgent. For a brief moment he bent forward and down and licked the length of the pink slit, sliding the rough hair between his teeth. She gasped and clutched for his head, but by then he was leaning over her. He pulled her towards him until her hips were at the seat edge, then thrust his cock forward. The pleasure and tightness of her cunt surprised him and he called out in relief. Her leg fell from the seat back and she clutched him to her loins with an unbreakable hold. Willingly he started sawing in and out. She was so tight she could have been a virgin, and as he clutched at her breast and filled her mouth with his tongue he felt himself thanking all the *kami* for his deliverance. They cried out together in the throes of orgasm. For Millicent this was the first time she had come to a climax in two years. The moisture of frustration and lust flooded from her interior and soaked into the plush bus seat. Kaoru felt her juices and spurted into her roughly, uncaring of the uncomfortable position. They clutched at one another convulsively as wave after wave blended their bodies together.

He raised his head from hers. "Are all *gaijin* women like you?" he asked shyly. "I have never had a woman so. . . ."

She shushed him with a kiss. "Don't move yet."

He noticed with surprise that her tight cunt was still holding his cock in a tight grip, and that he was as randy as he had been before. He started oscillating his ass, slowly, then with growing speed. "What is your name?" he gasped. She told him as her hands descended onto his muscular bottom to clutch him more deeply into herself.

In the middle seats, Andy was stroking Hana's full juicy cunt preparatory to entering her again. Her body writhed against his.

"Excuse me," a shadow loomed at them through the barely lit bus interior. "May I?" A hand reached out tentatively, stroking Hana's shoulder. "I would like. . . ."

She rose from against Andy's chest. "Of course," she said with complete courtesy. "Please, Andy-san, you will not mind?"

"Of course not," Andy said generously.

Her slim figure rose from the seat. All she wore were her shoes and Andy stroked the sticky inner skin of her thigh as she stepped over his legs. The young tourist raised the arm of the seat next to Andy and sat facing the aisle. His cock, stubby and fat, rose from a nest of wiry black hairs. His muscular brown stomach tensed with anticipation. Hana divined his intention immediately. She crouched over him. The young man seized her breasts and exerted a steady downward pressure. With two hands she guided the erect prick to her hungry moist hole. A beatific smile covered the young man's face and was reflected in Hana's. Andy observed them curiously, his own lust beginning to rise. Hana's eyes were open, the man's closed. He breathed harder as her exquisitely tight cunt descended, swallowing his entire length. At last he could feel the bones of her pubis mashed against the soft flesh of his stomach.

He drew a deep breath. "You are only the third woman I have had," he murmured. "So sweet. I had my wife and Mrs. Sato just a while ago. Wonderful, wonderful."

Andy peered towards the rear of the tour bus. Two women, both quite plump, both rather young were entwined around a young man. Andy vaguely remembered the two honeymooning couples that had been part of the tour. Presumably two of those in the rear seat were Satos, the other the wife of Hana's current lover.

Hana raised herself, her thigh muscles bunching, until she could feel the tip of the fat cock almost emerging from between her moist and hungry lips, then lowered herself again. The tourist squeezed her breasts, exploring them thoroughly with his fingers. Intrigued, Andy crouched in the aisle to examine the action. The floor light illuminated the juncture of the two bodies. As Hana rose Andy could see the lips and rim of her cunt distend with reluctance. As she descended the prick rammed into her with a growing fury. Andy parted her buns. She cast a perplexed but by no means forbidding look over her shoulder. He examined the motion from close up, the smells of the young woman's juices, and of the male essences that had poured into her, including his own, caused his own cock to rise. Drawn by the faint, earthy, bitter smell, he touched the tiny button of her anus. It had been wettened by the discharges that had rolled between her thighs as she sat against him. His forefinger was almost sucked inside, sliding through the muscular portal. Hana raised her face blindly, shoving out her ass to accommodate him without stopping her gentle ride on the man before her.

Andy pushed his exploring finger in to the knuckle. He twisted his hand about, revelling in the slick muscular feeling of her interior. Against his finger, more sensitive to touch than any cock, he could feel the male shaft through the tissues of her interior. He pulled his finger out slowly, twisting it about as he did so. Her breathing quickened, as did that of her mount. Andy pushed the man's thighs apart and stood between them. He bent his knees and held his raging red-tipped prick in one fist, prying apart the girl's buns with the other. In that uncomfortable position he pushed forward. The tip lodged in the crack of her ass, slid up and down until it found the brown hole. Hana leaned back, her body arched, ass and head extended backwards as in encouragement. Andy kissed her neck briefly then arced his body backwards to observe the progress he was making in her ass. The crown disappeared into the muscular entrance which distended and gripped the pulsing smooth shaft. It swallowed the flange then squeezed Andy's glans with a powerful grip. He shoved forward with his hips and watched as the shaft disappeared steadily into the welcoming hot hole.

Hana and the man had ceased moving as Andy made his way into her posterior. Once she felt the hairs at the base of Andy's cock, Hana attempted to move again. She raised herself off the two shafts, supporting herself by the seat backs on either side. Then carefully yet rapidly she lowered herself onto the two waiting meaty poles. Her two men aided her pleasure. The one in front by squeezing and moulding her breasts, the one behind, obviously the more experienced, by slipping his hand over her belly and fingering the top of her gorged slit and the soft wet nubbin that she knew as the seat of her pleasure. Her face was frozen as an ivory mask as she began repeating the motion, forcing the two male shafts, entirely dependent on her will, deeper and deeper into her body.

The position was excruciatingly uncomfortable for Andy. His knees were flexed in an unnatural position and he was constantly losing his balance as the girl's ass descended onto his extended cock. Gradually her rhythm quickened and her breathing with it. The man behind her was breathing harder, too, and by peering over her shoulder Andy could see that the hands on her breasts were mashing at the soft hills with a fierce demanding brutality that she was egging on with string fingernails driven into his skin.

The seated man began bucking and snorting as his climax approached. Andy too felt the rise of his pleasure, delayed only by the weakness and pain in his knees and back. The man beneath Hana cried out and forced his mouth against one of her nipples. She dug urgent nails into the nape of his neck, and extended her ass towards Andy. He pushed at the girl's back as he felt his own pleasure rising. She toppled the man she was riding and Andy thrust forcefully, once then again into her willing muscular interior. Her muscles contracted both fore and aft and squeezed copious flows of liquid from both men. Andy lay on top, his cock bathing in the liquid of his own discharge, panting heavily. At last the man at the bottom of the pile stirred. Andy pulled out his softening cock. Hana clenched her muscles in a vain dreamy effort to retain both morsels in her. A tiny shudder ran through her frame as a secondary orgasm took her.

She rose regretfully and walked through the bus to the toilet in the rear. Her training took over notwithstanding her naked state. All the passengers, she noted automatically, seemed to be well. The young man who had come with Andy was still occupied by the two mature women. The two women and man in the back were sleeping peacefully entwined. The driver was out of his seat but she could see his legs entwined with those of the *gaijin* woman's. Other men were sleeping peacefully on the seats. professionally she was glad this was only the start of the season and there were no more people to care for. But her sticky cunt sent messages of regret that there were not many more cocks to be tried on this special night.

# CHAPTER 13:

# WON'T YOU HAVE ANOTHER PIECE?

The bus driver reassumed his seat and Hana, the pretty tour guide addressed the microphone with gloved hand and lowered eyes.

"The bus company and we the crew of the bus apologize with all sincerity for last night's breakdown. We realize that this is inexcusable. Those of the honorable passengers who wish to resume the tour may do so, the company also invites all of you to a picnic, provided by the company in partial compensation for the trouble you have suffered. We hope you will accept this offer and our apologies, too." She raised her head, saw Andy's gaze on hers, blushed slightly, and lowered her eyes again. "We will make a special stop at Hanagahara lookout point for the picnic. I hope you enjoy yourselves and are able to forgive us."

The rescue teams had arrived from the Takayama side early in the morning. They had driven to a small town

*170*

along the route where the bus company had provided for all of them to stay at an inn. The storm had passed and a warm breeze was melting the snow even at their altitude. Some of the passengers: the two anonymous businessmen the middle-aged couple, and the missionary, had taken an earlier bus. Kaoru, the driver, treasured a handwritten card with Millicent's address in his breast pocket. His cock glowed every time he felt the stiff cardboard.

Two men and a young woman had joined the trip. Both were elderly and did not spare the other passengers a glance. They did not know what the special trip was for, but by the grins under their sunglasses it was obvious they enjoyed the prospect of a freebee.

They passed through the tunnel of the previous night's adventure, and there were many reminiscent smiles on the faces that peered out of the windows. Hanagahara proved to be an exquisite lookout point well off the regular route. It provided a view of a deep valley and its surrounding mountains.

They parked the bus and the guide and driver unloaded the makings of a lavish picnic. Andy sat on the *goza* mat only partly absorbed in the *bento* tray before him. Bits of fish, meat, and vegetables had been arranged in the lacquered compartments with due attention to harmonizing texture, color, and flavor. His eyes crossed those of Hana. She blushed and lowered her gaze. The lustful magic of the previous evening seemed a thing of the past, and yet . . . He smiled at her.

Still absorbed in his memory of the previous night, Andy strolled along the meadow. He came upon the two women he had seen with Jim the previous night. They were looking at the view and exchanging complacent remarks about the beauty of the place. For a moment, their faces to the sun and his in shadow, they mistook him for Jim. Their faces lit up and they waved him to their side.

"Ah!" Tsuya said. "I thought you are Jimmu-san."

"No. I'm his brother . . ."

They looked at one another in perplexity. Then an unvoiced message seemed to flash between the two women. "Would you like to sit with us?" Fumiko asked gaily.

Andy bowed. "Of course. With two such lovely companions . . ."

They laughed kittenishly. He flopped down on the ground beside them. Fumiko fumbled in the lush grass beside them.

"Do *gaijin* drink sake?" Tsuya asked with a girlish giggle, ignoring the plastic cup in Andy's hand.

"Sometimes," he said grinning at them.

"Then we will offer you some," Fumiko tittered, holding up one of the bottles of sake the guide had dispensed from the bus.

"But not here!" Tsuya's lips clamped grimly, though the laughter was still evident in the corner of her eyes. "No, not here. There is a better place for drinking sake. Come on *gaijin*-san." She rose unsteadily to her feet. Obviously she had been enjoying the bus company's hospitality to the limit.

Giggling conspiratorially, the two women led Andy into a tiny hollow surrounded by bushes. On one side the hollow opened to reveal the full sweep of the valley and the mountain opposite. Looking across Andy realized that the white structure he could see quite clearly was the mansion he and Jim had seen indistinctly some days before: the same as the one pictured on the bottle of perfume essence May McCormick said came from the Clouds and Rain Corporation. Still staring at the mysterious mansion he was pulled back onto his back, his head resting comfortably on Tsuya's lap.

Fumiko's hands were fumbling at his fly. His cock sprang erect and the two women contemplated his erection. "Just like the other one's." one of the women said.

"Maybe they are brothers after all?" another voice said doubtfully.

"I'll taste and tell you."

"Let's both taste and compare."

His head was laid gently on a folded sweater. Two pairs of lips engulfed his cock. At first they nibbled tentatively at either sides of the stick. Then gradually their experimentation took a more lustful tone. He felt the tip, then the shaft of the cock inserted into each demanding mouth in turn. His balls were subject to minute attention as tongue flicks probed its soft silky surface. They alternated, one mouth sucking at the knob, the other occupied with his balls. Andy felt himself helpless in their grip. The mountain sun was warming his eyes behind closed lids, and his limbs were growing heavy. So too was his cock, which after all the attention it had received resembled a glowing iron bar. His hips started jerking minutely and he knew the tiny transparent drop had appeared at the tip. The two women murmured to one another between tastes of his malehood.

The sun was obscured by a shadow and he found his nose and mouth occupied by the steamy heat of a woman's pussy. Automatically his tongue licked out. The woman moved over him, adjusting her position. Then her hands were over his face, opening her nether lips to allow his tongue easier access. Andy licked with a will, notwithstanding the lassitude of his limbs as his cock was licked continuously by two expert mouths. Then he felt the length of the shaft engulfed by a demanding and knowledgable throat. Lips nibbled at the hairs of his crotch. He wondered hazily, as he continued thrusting his tongue forward, how she was able to encompass the length. The soft hairy skin of his scrotum was pulled up by another pair of lips, then one of his balls was sucked gently into a warm cavern. The mouths withdrew as their owners changed position.

There was a flash of sunlight and the taste of the lips above him changed. He licked at her once again. This time his cock was cushioned by the fullness of female breasts and he jogged himself lightly within the imprisoning flesh pillows. The last thing he could remember was the eruption of his cock against the softness of two female breasts just as his tongue brought on a flood of juices from the warm cunt he was engaged in.

Jim wandered through the meadow looking for Andy. Though the lust of the previous night had worn off, there was still a feeling of tension in the small group. The two honeymooning couples had wandered off, as had Fumiko and Tsuya. He paused at the edge of the meadow. Looking across the valley he spied the low wide outlines of a white building. Now he knew there was something very wrong. He stared at the structure for a moment, then turned to find Andy. Instead of his brother he found himself bumping into the severely dressed young woman who had boarded the bus that morning. He started to apologize. She smiled, and then her red-painted lips were reaching for his mouth. Her frame clung to his own and her tongue filled his mouth.

Jim as so surprised he started to fall. Rather than supporting him she let him drop, and they ended with her straddling him. The blood was pounding in his ears and to his surprise he found himself with a massive erection. Still wearing her enigmatic smile the young woman raised herself above his hips. She unzipped his fly without any hesitation and produced his cock, then sat on it, probing for her own slit with the blunt knob.

They both sighed as the shaft disappeared inside her body. She crouched over him without a word, shaking her hips from side to side, then kissed him again. Jim tasted a faint bitterness on her tongue. He tried to pull away, but she pursued him with a greedy certainty. Without a pause she rode him to a climax. His hips arced off the ground, filling her pussy to the best of his ability, clawing at her skirted thighs with stiff fingers. His body was controlling itself, and his conscious mind noted the approach of the two men who had joined the bus in the morning. They smiled enigmatically, and as the pulsing of his orgasm ended, Jim dropped into unconsciousness knowing his premonitions had not been mistaken.

# CHAPTER 14:

# INTO THE JAWS

The young woman in the severe suit and the open lab coat examined the two of them clinically without saying a word.

"Good specimens," she said, turning to one of her companions. Their faces were in the dark, but both were rather heavy set men.

"They'll do."

The voice was somehow familiar. Andy suddenly recalled where he had heard it before. It was the voice of the man in the bus, the older man with greying hair who had joined the tour bus on the second day after the landslide.

"Try it on them," the voice directed enigmatically, then the two men turned and walked away.

The woman, scientist? doctor? guard? examined them thoroughly with her eyes for a long moment. Jim struggled to rise only to discover that the drug that had been used on him was still powerful. He fell back, his muscles jelly-like. He recognized the woman as the one who had trapped him at the meadow, and wondered peripherally what had happened to the rest of the tour.

Andy examined the woman who was examining them. Her short cropped hair gave her face an elfine look. She was without makeup—unusual in a Japanese woman—and, he decided, quite beautiful, but for the cold passionless look in her eye.

They were lying side by side in a room that combined the appearance of an advanced chemical laboratory, an alchemist's dungeon, and a comfortable sitting room. One entire wall of the room was lined with shelves, and the shelves were filled with bottles of various shapes and sizes. Some appeared to be bottles of commercial perfumes, others bore the hallmark of the laboratory. There was an expensive persian rug in one corner and a wood panelled library. Several computers and electronic devices; a sinister looking laboratory bench on which reposed several nondescript vials and bottles. And two doorways, the use of either of which would have suited Jim and Andy just fine. They were both nude, lying on gurneys but not strapped down.

Andy's head flopped back, exhausted by his survey of the room. The young woman had just finished attaching several instruments to various parts of their bodies. She worked with cool impersonality, even when she attached probes, using adhesive, to their flaccid cocks.

Jim tried to signal his brother with his eyes, but the effort was too great. In any case, there was no sense in planning anything: they simply were unable to move. The young woman fussed with her instruments, some of which hummed and buzzed, most of which gave no visible reaction. She returned to survey their prone forms with a professional eye. Then she took each of the penises in her hands and began stroking them in measured cadence. To his amazement, Andy felt himself responding to her ministrations. The feeling was dimmed, as if at some remove, but his cock rose at her command with a will of its own. She examined the erection at hands length, then compared them by bringing her face as close as she could. Jim imagined he could feel her warm breath on the shaft. An amused look crossed her face and she shook the two staves in the air, banging them against the men's bellies. Then she smiled wickedly at the two paralyzed men and walked over to the lab bench. She selected one of the bottles. This time as she walked there was nothing impersonal about her movements. Her hips swayed beneath the formal black suit and there was an obvious glint in her eyes.

The vial contained an odorless jellylike substance. She poured some of it into each hand, juggling the vial carefully, then started rubbing the erect cocks again. To Jim and Andy the effect was as if they had had their cocks rubbed free of skin so that the nerve ends themselves were exposed. Andy looked down in panic and was relieved to see that the stuff had not peeled his cock bare. Within a few minutes of her ministrations, it seemed as if their cocks had become iron bars, glowing with heat and expanding as she worked.

When she was satisfied, she casually dropped her lab coat and climbed on to one of the gurneys. Jim stared hypnotized as she raised her skirt and exposed a pert bottom and shaven pussy lips. She squatted and lowered herself over his erection, guiding it into the sweet hole without ado and allowing her weight to sink the shaft into her depths. Both her hands rested on his helpless chest and she began pumping at him, raising herself to the tip, then dropping down again. A dreamy look came into her eyes and she alternated fingering her clitoral bud with scratching more and more violently at Jim's chest muscles.

For Jim the sensation was akin to the first time he had ever had sex. He could feel his pulse racing and the exquisite sensation of a female tube wrapped around him was enough to bring tears to his eyes. He wanted to call out, to use his mouth and hands, and he raged against his helplessness. He could feel every corrugation of her internal canal, every dip and sweet hollow of her. As the speed of her movements increased so did his detachment from his own body and his focusing on the sensations his penis was sending to his brain. Finally he was dimly conscious that he had turned purely into a male principle. The center of his universe was the slick fusion of his body into hers, and the rest of the world receded to a dim nothingness.

The eruption, when it came, was like nothing he had ever felt before. It rose from the soles of his feet, gathering speed up his spine to his head, then focused down again to his testicles. Waves of orgasm rushed through his blood stream erupting into her waiting interior. He managed to focus his eyes in time to see the pulsing of his cock into her and the residue of his cream flow out over her distended lips. For one second she smiled brilliantly at him, then her face returned to its previous impassivity.

Jim watched as she rose from him. Her scant black hairs were dappled with the froth from his balls. He watched in envy as she straddled Andy and commenced fucking him. Slowly at first, then going faster, she raised and lowered herself with abandon on his brother's supine and helpless body. She reached a second climax, then milked Andy of his juices. Andy's face bore a look of slack, mechanical calm until the final seconds of his orgasm, then blazed forth with a lustful frenzy even the drug could not contain.

She stepped away from them and smoothed her dress, then picked up her lab coat and walked out of the room.

The two were left, side by side on their gurneys, inside a circle of brilliant white light. With an effort Andy managed to move his lips.

"Wha' hell happn?" he mumbled.

"Trap," Jim managed to say.

"Gotta ge' out."

"Yeah. How?"

Their labored conversation was interrupted by two female figures. They too wore lab coats, though they were not the twins' original interlocutor. They seemed pleasantly, though not overly surprised at the sight, as if they met with two helpless naked men wearing nothing but huge erections in the normal course of their day. They spoke to one another quickly, then approached the two helpless figures.

One of them sucked on Andy's cock, Again he felt the river of lava run down the shaft to his testicles. She played with his cock, stroking the length with her fingers and tongue and raising the full bag. The other disdained such niceties. She dropped her panties and raised her lab coat, then climbed up and seated herself on Jim's helpless body. The other woman, slightly older, watched as her companion began ramming herself furiously onto Jim's helpless body. She gave one final suck at Andy's cock, then mounted him as well.

For the two men the sensations were much as they had been before. The intensity was so great Jim knew he had passed out at the final act, as his sperm rushed through his extended cock. Andy too seemed mentally bruised by the encounter. The two women finished and stepped off their victims. The older one kissed Andy's cock in passing, the one who had ridden Jim merely walked away, rebuttoning her coat.

"What the hell is going on?" Jim found that the original

drug was slowly wearing off. He could raise his neck now, though from the neck down he was till paralyzed, with one important exception.

"I don't know," Andy groaned. "We gotta get out of here before this kills us."

"I could try pulling myself off this bier with my teeth."

"Funnies I get. Let's wait until it wears off completely. Don't show it's wearing off. Maybe we'll be able to do something."

They were interrupted again. Two women this time as well. One of them had large breasts which she used to stimulate Jim's cock, and presumably herself, before mounting him. She winked at Jim as he watched the tip of his cock appear and disappear into her cleavage. When she had finished, she bent and kissed him deeply and lovingly. He wished he could respond, but pretended the paralysis was still complete. She watched complacently as her companion rode to a climax aboard Andy. Jim's fluids seeped down her thighs and stuck to his belly so that there was an audible sucking sound as she rose off his still erect prick.

"How's it now?" Jim asked when the two had left.

"I can wriggle my fingers," Andy said.

They had little time to experiment. Another woman came in and helped herself. First to Andy, then when she had erupted to her own satisfaction, she mounted Jim and rode to a second climax. They had barely recovered when another two women entered the room. One of them was the short-haired severe woman who had anointed them first. She checked her instruments, then unhurriedly joined the other who was riding dreamily on Andy. The two men watched helplessly as the women used their fingers on their own and on the men's bodies. They compared their mounts in great detail, then giggled as they switched from one man to the other to confirm their comparisons. Andy's climax was as strong as it had been before. This time, however, he managed to retain some of his rationality as his body jerked helplessly in the throes of passion. His forearm and toes seemed to have been released from thrall, and he wondered whether his body would give out from exhaustion before or after the drug freed him.

A man entered the room. He was young and bore a studious look. Seeing the two women he asked politely if he may join. The gamine beauty waved him to her. He dropped his pants and climbed onto the gurney. She bent forward to accommodate him, and Andy watched from the side as the strangers cock disappeared slowly into the woman's cunt alongside Jim's. The second insertion tightened the cunt that was imprisoning Jim's cock considerably. Unable to move he felt the man's cock as it fucked into the woman along with his own. All three of them jerked on the bier until the man agitated his ass rapidly and spewed a stream of come, liberally bedewing Jim and the woman's cunt. At the same time Jim felt the incredible rush of his own orgasm start again and he spiralled down into darkness.

They woke in a luxurious Japanese-style room. Sunlight glowed behind the clean new *shoji*. Andy felt himself. His cock had returned to its normal dimensions. He sat up in bed and nudged his brother who was stirring on a nearby *futon*. Jim sat up with a groan. "What the hell happened?" he asked.

"They just fucked us all night, I guess," Andy answered.

"I think I passed out."

"A couple of times. Me, too. What the hell *was* that stuff? I could make a fortune from it."

"Would you? Or more properly, should you?" Jim was staring thoughtfully at his brother.

Andy thought hard for a moment. "Noooo. I guess I couldn't, could I? What now?"

"Breakfast," Jim said forcefully. Just then they heard "Please, food is served," from behind the sliding *fusuma* doors at one side of the room.

They found folded *yukata* at the feet of the bedding. In the other room were footed lacquer trays set for two. A steaming tea kettle to one side.

The food restored their strength.

"Nothing like shrimp for breakfast," Jim said luxuriously. The large steamed crustacean stared back at him with beady eyes. Little plates containing cooked vegetables and seaweeds, rice, soup, pickles, and fish and the inevitable raw egg disappeared quickly. Over a final cup of tea they smiled and lolled back.

"Now what?" Jim asked rhetorically.

*"Gomen kudasai,"* their council of war was interrupted before it had even properly begun. The *fusuma* slid open. Their chief interlocutor of the previous night stood there demurely. The two tried to rise to their feet, Jim groping hastily for his chopsticks as a weapon. There was a hint of a smile in the short-haired young woman's lips.

"Fine-sensei and Kitamura-sensei would like to speak to you, if you're ready. Your clothes are in the other room. I will wait outside." She bowed and slid the *fusuma* shut again.

"She could have left the door open. We've no secrets from her anyway," Andy grouched.

*"Fine*-sensei? Kitamura-sensei?" Jim looked from the closed door to Andy. "What the hell is going on here?"

"We'll never know till we find out, will we?" They headed for the other room at speed.

She was waiting as they opened the door. A long polished-wood corridor was before them.

"My name is Mayumi," she said sweetly. "I am Fine-sensei's assistant, and also administrative manager of one of the projects."

The two nodded as if they understood as she led them through the mansion, then bade them enter a heavy wooden door.

The room was furnished in Japanized Western style. Comfortable sofas and low tables were scattered throughout on a thick carpet. There was a large liquor cabinet, as well as several modern Japanese-style pictures in a purple hue that Jim recognized from his and Andy's single original painting. One side of the room was dominated by a large picture window that looked out over a formal Japanese garden and to the green clad mountains beyond.

Two men stood in the center of the room. Both were beyond middle-age, rather plump. Both wore glasses and had the relaxed yet worried expression of company executives. One was Japanese, his face rounded and creased with smile wrinkles. His greenish eyes almost hidden by the folds of his eyelids. The other was European, and he wore the distracted aura of a baby peering out at the world for the first time.

"I'm Kitamura Dansuke."

"I am Leonard Fine." They spoke at the same instant. The four men stared at one another uneasily for a long moment. Now that the moment had come, none of them knew how to act.

"Shall I pour some tea?" Mayumi's voice broke into the silence.

Fine motioned the two young men to a seat on a sofa besides the window. He and Kitamura seated themselves opposite Jim and Andy in two armchairs.

"Well?" Andy's voice was cold. "Would you like to explain? I imagine you," he pointed to Fine, "are my long-lost natural father, whatever that means. Whereas you," he pointed to Kitamura who blinked behind his glasses, "have been hounding us all the way from Tokyo, and you were on the bus as well, disguised with dark glasses. . . ."

"Actually," Kitamura said in perfect English, "you forgot to mention that I am likely the father of one or both of you as well."

"I am supposed to have the honor of claiming you?" Jim asked. There was acid in his voice. "What is the point of all of this?"

"First of all, to get to know you of course," Fine said.

"You could have written us a letter," Jim snapped.

Fine made soothing noises and Mayumi poured some tea then retired to the background.

"There was a purpose to all of this," Kitamura said half apologetically. Fine slouched in the armchair at his side, beaming at them like a demented teddy bear. "Consider for a moment how you reacted in the last night. Notwithstanding the *fugu* derivative we had paralyzed you with, and what you probably thought was an imminent and certain threat to your lives, you kept on pumping."

"Humping," Fine corrected his partner.

"Don't you find that a little bit strange? And the incident in the bus? And the night before at the *onsen?*"

"I saw you there, didn't I?" Jim suddenly exclaimed, pointing at Leonard Fine. "I walked in while you were making love. . . ."

Fine grinned. "I had been testing SP15, spraying it as an aerosol, and stopped to enjoy the benefits. Seeing you at the entrance to that room startled me, let me tell you. Luckily you were already under the influence. Kitty placed a small time-set aerosol in the bus just before it left as well.''

"Of what?" Jim asked.

"This." Kitamura held up a peculiar vial. It was a cubic crystal block that had been hollowed out, producing a bottle with very thick walls. Inside reposed about a teaspoonful of pink liquid. The stopper to the bottle was almost as large as the container and seemed to contain several valves. "Very volatile. SP15. Series fifteen of a human sex pheromone. Open this bottle, and in the absence of a female we'd all be trying to poke holes through the walls in search of a female human. *Very* specific." He put the vial down.

"And goddamn dangerous," Fine added gloomily. "Can you imagine what could be done with that stuff? We spread less than a microgram in the bus that night."

Jim and Andy looked at the bottle with respect.

"This still doesn't explain all the rigamarole, and the guys sent to scare us away and all," Andy said forcefully. "*And* last night."

"Well, last night . . ." Fine wriggled uneasily in his seat. "That was a bit of a joke really. Though we did want you to have an idea of the effects first-hand."

"Some joke," Jim sneered, though he could not forebear a grin. The humor of the situation did tickle his fancy.

"The whole thing *is* related, including the men who tried scaring you off. And we actually did not send all of them. The Typhon have been active as well. Some of the private eyes we have hired have had a sharp time disposing of them. Remember the two *yakuza* who got into your apartment. It's true you dealt with them, I don't know how, but they would have returned without some persua-

sion from us," Fine said uneasily. He turned to Kitamura.
"You explain it, Kitty."

"We might as well start from the beginning. Does the
name Typhon mean anything to you?"

The two younger men stiffened. "I don't mean Mary,
your mother. We'll come to that in a minute. No, there's
a family by that name. They have business interests,
mainly in Europe. Never heard of them? Jim? They're in
computers, too. Andy? You're the businessman . . ."

They both shook their heads.

"Goes to show, doesn't it?"

The two nodded, though still not comprehending.

"Five years after World War II, I was a foreign corre-
spondent for a Japanese newspaper. I went to the US to
write a series of articles. In California I met a fascinating
young woman, Mary Typhon. We made love, often, and
apparently, in the intervals, while I was away, she was
also having an affair with a young chemistry student."

"Me," said Fine thumbing his chest. "And she was
the best piece I had ever had. I was madly in love with
her."

"As was I," Kitamura continued quietly. "Anyway,
the Korean war broke out. I was ordered to Korea to
cover it from the American side because I spoke good
English. . . ."

"Atrocious English," Fine said, "but his bosses were
hardly able to judge as they were unable to speak it themselves . . ."

Kitamura grinned and continued. "I met Lenny in Pusan
market. He had been drafted into the Navy, and spent his
time examining native chemicals long before it became the
fashion. We became friends through a Korean lady . . ."

"Neither of us could afford her on his own. Really, she
was a first class *kisaeng* and both of us were desperate,"

Fine interjected. "The three of us had a wonderful time when I was in port."

"She liked both of us, not the least because I could speak Korean and Lenny used some of his spices."

"Very crude I was in those days: pepper and camphor, and other traditional things." Fine smiled reminiscently.

"The long and the short of it is we started thinking about things. Lenny knew more about smells than anyone I ever knew, and I had some ideas about marketing. We started manufacturing perfume essence after I borrowed some money, made a go of it, and here we are."

"Along the way I started getting interested in phermonones. Know what they are? Complex molecules that affect organisms directly . . ."

"Like ants?" Jim asked.

"Exactly. Well human beings are less susceptible to pheromones than most animals, but if you know the trick . . . Well, you saw the effect."

"And you can imagine what thoughtless, or malevolent use of the stuff could do," Kitamura chipped in.

"We also, because of our family connection and mutual hobby, you might say, got interested in the general psychology and physiology of sex. A combination of chemical and physiological results you wouldn't believe." Fine smiled widely. "Actually, considering your performance to date, and your antecedents, you probably would."

"And what about *us*," Jim asked.

"Well, during and immediately after the war we were too busy to think of Mary. Only much later, by chance, we discovered we were each the 'other man' in our mutual lives. By then Mary had disappeared. Her records wiped, presumably by the Typhons themselves. We found out about you two only when you reached adolescence. And we did what we could, which was not much. By then we were already on a collision course with the Typhon enterprises. When you each arrived independently in Japan we decided to get you to met one another, and then, later, to meet us.''

"Why not just come in politely and knock on our door?" Jim persisted.

"There's something else, isn't there?" Andy asked thoughtfully.

The two older men nodded. "Yes," they said in unison, and then Lenny let his partner speak. "First, the matter of the pheromone. Lenny has been working on it for years now. And in the past ten years, the Typhons have started taking an interest. From what we could gather, they are not particularly pleasant people. Frankly, the stuff is *so* dangerous, we don't know what to do with it. But from what we know of the Typhons, they'd just as likely market it, or use it for their ends, which, as far as we can gather, are rather unsociable. So we needed someone to share the decision, someone younger, and who better than a relative? Second, we wanted to see what you two were made of. Nepotism is all good and well, but it can lead to the destruction of all our efforts. Finally, the Typhons are also interested in you, for reasons we can't comprehend, and we didn't want their attention directed to the potential tie between us.''

Andy sank back into his chair. "Well, I can hardly feel the urge to throw myself into your arms and call you 'Daddy,' Mr. Fine.''

Fine smiled his teddy bear smile again. He was struggling for the right words when Kitamura interjected with a grin. "And it might be highly inappropriate. You see, biologically at least, you may not be his, but mine. We tend to think of you both as our joint effort. *Our* sons, if you will. Of course, if you are really interested in parentage, we can always have a gene scan made. Len and I have the same blood type you see, so a simple blood test would not be sufficient.''

"I don't look Japanese, Jim does," Andy objected.

"Tsk tsk. Stereotyping from a smart young man like you. Actually, Mary, your mother, looked like an oriental . . .''

"Or an Indian . . .''

"Same thing. Without a gene analysis, we couldn't tell for certain. Both of you could easily pass as either European or Asian.''

"Stop teasing the boys, Kitty. I don't care which of you is the product of my balls, if either. I love you both and as far as I'm concerned, you're part of the family, whatever you or that fat buddha in the chair there thinks.'' Fine rose and affectionately rubbed Andy and Jim's heads. "I'm glad you're here, and that's enough.'' Kitamura nodded sagely in the background.

"You'll stay here for a while. We'll get to know one another.'' Fine headed for the door. "Make good use of your time.'' He winked and was gone.

# CHAPTER 15:

# TRAITOR TO THE CAUSE

Omi Hanako peered doubtfully through the binoculars. The powerful glasses made the scene shift rapidly. They gave her a headache. The grounds of the traditionally-designed mansion she was spying on were filling up in the late afternoon. Many of the workers lived about the place, which was odd though not completely unknown in the Japanese corporate world. The gardens that surrounded the mansions and its outbuildings—acres of carefully crafted terraces, miniature waterways and rocky forests—touched a sense of beauty deep in her soul. She had become more aware of such bourgeois things since the start of the year. Others had noticed her attitude, and her commune leader had insisted on her coming along on this expedition to attack the capitalist imperialist forces in their lair. It was clear even to her newly rebellious awareness that *something* odd was going on at the rural headquarters of the Clouds and Rain Corporation. Too many people seemed to live on the premises, the security was excessive even for a normally secretive Japanese company, and there were no signs of the usual ugly barracklike buildings that characterized most Japanese research labs. Instead, it appeared, the corporate bosses spent time and energy in decorating their surroundings and making their headquarters as traditional as possible. The grey tiled roofs, the white walls and brown woodwork all merged perfectly into the side of the mountain. She raised the binoculars again. Two figures had appeared on one of the terraces near one of the many outbuildings that composed the mansion.

There was something familiar about the two figures on the terrace. She tried to adjust the focus to get a better picture, shook her head angrily when she failed. The two figures were alike in build, size, and even in the way they stood. This more than anything brought a faint glimmering of recognition to her mind. It was only when one of the figures stood in profile that she recognized Andy Middler. She smiled softly to herself in memory. She had met Middler and Suzuki after Andy had saved her from being attacked by ideological rivals. Unconsciously her free hand stole to her crotch. The touch of the rough camouflage fabric of her jacket brought cruel reality crashing back. She bit her lip in worried thought. She had had no particular emotions about what she, and others, were about to do, but this was different. She owed Middler and Suzuki too much. And once again she felt a wetness between her thighs at the thought of making love to both of the young men simultaneously. In her limited experience of lovemaking, and plentiful experience of sex, the two were among the few who had taught her about the former.

"Hey, Omi, come here," a rough voice called to her in a whisper.

She obediently crawled down from her tree perch. It

was Numajiri, whose cold eyes observed and used her form with as much lack of emotion as they viewed a killing. She, and most of the others in the action group as well, were terrified of the radical leader of the Committee for Capitalist Eradication.

"We will have an ideological self-examination session, and then finalize our plans," he said gruffly. He always spoke in those tones, not just to her. It was when his voice turned quiet and measured that killings began. She wished, not for the first time in the most recent months, that she had never embarked on this life. She thought again of her parents' small apartment in Osaka, and of the caring they hid behind their hardworking lives.

The self-examination session she found as boring as always in the recent past. Once, she knew, she would have been as attentive as anyone else, just now, however. . . .

The men discussed their plans. The women, as usual, listened silently. Only Maki, the firebrand, corrected them on points of ideological purity. There were ten members of the group, three of them women. This time Numajiri's plan seemed foolproof. Using explosives and pyrotechnics, they were going to penetrate the heart of the capitalist pigs' fortress. They would capture what documents they could for later publication and denunciation and burn the mansion to the ground. Anyone who stood in their way, well, Ito, the fanatical leader of her own Hammer contingent made a squashing motion with his thumb. They were all armed with iron bars and Ito, among his talents, was wizard with electronic and chemical devices. Which meant lots of bombs. In this case the reliance on electronic warning measures and the lack of armed guards was going to cost the fascist running dogs dearly. The first step, however, was penetrating the traditional seeming white-washed wall which ran around the mansion's grounds. It was two meters tall and topped with a traditional tile combing, like a tiny pitched roof. "Traditional seeming" because they had seen the sheen of alarm wires running along its length.

"Someone is going to have to go and plant the explosive at the wall before the attack," the leader of the Star group said. He was a powerful young man whom in other circumstances—bathed and shaved—Omi would have found attractive. But his lovemaking, she remembered, left much to be desired.

Numajiri flattened the aerial photo they had had taken of the area and enlarged at a commercial lab in Tokyo. "The gate is protected by electronic means, and we are unable to penetrate it. The same goes for the wall. The approaches are also under surveillance by video cameras in mobile housings along the walls. We've identified one place that *might* not be under observation." He pointed to a place on the air photo. "Right here. There's a small gully right here. Maybe twenty centimeters deep, maybe thirty in some places. Someone very slim might be able to slip along the depression without being observed by the cameras."

Ito looked at her sideways. Hanako knew she was under trial here. She was far from being the most active ideologically in her own commune, and was surprised when the commune leader had chosen her to be part of the assault group. But it became clear in the two days they had spent in the forest that she was expected to prove herself ideologically. Or not to return at all.

"I'll go," she said simply. Ito seemed to relax a trifle. He handed her a heavy green day pack and a small black box.

"This is a radio transmitter," Numajiri said. "Push it, and you have five minutes to get out of the way, then it blows. To arm it you have to pull this ring here." He showed her a small copper ring attached to a wire inside the pack. "Don't lose the control."

She turned the box in her hands warily. It appeared to be a simple remote control, such as that used for a garage.

Numajiri grinned. "Yes, capitalist technology is so useful. And so available. Now go with Ito!"

"Now?" she asked in surprise.

"Yes, of course now. We want you to get into position."

Ito led her to the edge of the forest, several hundred meters away from the walls of the mansion. The dolphins on the main building's roof glinted in the reddish afternoon sunlight. The meadow that led from the forest to the wall smelled fresh and lush. Tiny flowers swayed in the light breeze.

"Now remember," Ito said to her, his eyes flashing behind his glasses. "We attack at dawn. You can't return the way you came. It's too risky. You will set of the charge the minute you see us attacking." Hanako nodded obsequiously. "You start now. There's no point in waiting until dark: they have thermal snoopers."

She nodded and headed off towards the meadow and the indicated spot where the depression started. For a moment she paused to look back. Ito was staring after her, an unreadable expression on his face. She shivered inwardly, realizing suddenly that she wanted to thwart the mad scheme but there did not seem to be any way out.

She hefted the pack again and continued up the mountain. She dared not approach the gate directly to warn the occupants. She was being observed by the group, and the gate guards would not have opened for her ragged figure in any case. She dropped to the ground behind a bush and tied the pack to her leg as instructed, then started crawling along the depression. Tall grass helped hide her as she snaked along. Her paint-splashed jeans jacket tore at the elbows and she felt the material at her knees go as well. Once she heard a rustle in the grass before her and she froze, fearing a viper. The pack caught on every imaginable obstacle and she sobbed beneath her breath trying to free it with desperate tugs of her foot.

The wall caught her by surprise and she barely kept in her scream. Raising her head she saw the tile overhang of the wall above her head, and jutting slightly forward, the barrel of a video camera.

Hanako flattened herself against the wall and examined her bruises and pains by feel. Pulling the satchel towards her, she placed it against the wall. The feel of the bag was repugnant. She could no longer remember what had motivated her to join the Central Struggle Committee. The days of her youth—all of two years before—and her youthful revolutionary zeal seemed so far away and out of place. She crawled along the wall, wanting to get as far as possible from the deadly pack.

Her shoulder pushing against the wall found a soft place in the structure. She examined the plaster cautiously. There were thin cracks in the white surface and some light seemed to come through. She pushed it with more confidence. An entire panel moved. It was the work of a moment for her to extract her small pocket knife and find the edge of the panel. Twisting and forcing the blade she found the wooden wedges that held the panel in place. The panel fell inwards silently and she followed it, a small muddy figure in torn clothing to face the expectant faces of two women and a man.

"Andy-san," she gasped gratefully. "They are coming to attack you."

Lenny Fine chuckled when she repeated her story. He looked at his partner and said, "Kitty, you were absolutely

right. Every fortress should have an obvious weakness."
He laughed again.

Kitamura beamed with pleasure, looking more than ever
like a fat almond eyed cat. "We have had you under
observation since you started crawling along that path-
way," he explained to Hanako. "It's wired of course.
Any attacker would use that not-so-obvious route." He
beamed again, and Hanako felt an atavistic urge to offer
thanks to the *kami*.

"What would you like to do now?" Kitamura asked.
"Aside from a bath, I mean. And the food out there in
the forest can't be terribly good either." He beamed at
her. She tried to see any maliciousness or delayed cruelty
in his voice, but his foreign-accented Japanese was full of
genuine warmth and concern. They were seated in a large
comfortable room furnished in Western style. After so
many days in the open, the deep armchair she was in
seemed obscenely relaxing.

"What are you going to do about the Committee?" she
asked tremulously. "Call the police?"

"Of course not!" Kitamura was genuinely surprised.
"They are harmless."

"Harmless?" she almost shrieked. Suddenly she realized that her own life was on the line as well. Her defec-
tion would not go unnoticed, and the various factions of
the Committee, including her own commune, had notori-
ous ways of dealing with defectors. Tears blinded her
eyes, compounded of fear and frustration.

"At least to us," Fine said in his carefully articulated
Japanese. "They would have been fatal to you. I've examined the rig they gave you. The goddamn remote was only
a backup."

"I don't understand," she said, but a dark certainty was
growing in her mind.

"There was a little brass ring you said you were supposed to pull? To release the safety?" His eyes were suddenly cold. "That was no safety. It would have blown you to kingdom come. The bastards," he added *sotto voce,* "such a waste of a beautiful young person." He spoke normally again. "Well, never matter, they'll be dealt with. You can watch, along with Jim and Andy. Actually, why don't you go along with them? They know the place well enough and will take good care of you." The three of them recognized the last as a dismissal and headed for the young men's quarters.

The walk through the mansion was balm to Hanako. It had been long since she had been conscious enough of her surroundings to enjoy beauty, and traditional beauty at that, for its own sake. She was suddenly conscious of her grubby clothes and appearance, and how it contrasted with the quiet wood and paper elegance of the corridors they passed. It was too late for many people to be about in the compound, but they all seemed cheerful and relaxed, not at all like the tenseness expressed by the stance of most modern Japanese. Including, she reminded herself, her own former comrades.

The *furo* bath was large enough for three, and she found without surprise that three was what it was going to hold. Jim and Andy undressed themselves first, forbidding her to move. She looked at the two young male bodies critically. They were less lean than the men of her commune, and their bones were well covered. But they were clean, and obviously enjoyed taking their time and parading before her. She looked at both of them, and there was little to choose between them. Their cocks, she knew, would be ready for her, firm and erect, when she would be ready. At the moment, however, she needed a bath, and waited impatiently for the next act. Andy started unbuttoning her man's shirt, and Jim addressed himself to her jeans.

"Hey, hang on a second," Jim said. He patted her pocket and extracted her small pocket knife, which she had absentmindedly found and placed back in her hip pocket once she had opened the wall.

Hanako's nervousness returned. Surely they would not think. . . .

Jim grinned wickedly, then winked at her reassuringly. "You're not going back to that mob?" he asked seriously.

"No. Never!" she said in horror and genuine dismay.

"Good. Then we have to dispose of your previous life." He flipped open the blade. It slit through the fabric at her shoulders, following the seams with some difficulty. The shirt dropped away from her, exposing her breasts and taut belly. Andy who had noticed her fright stroked her hair reassuringly while helping his brother with much laughter dispose of her clothes. Her jeans came next. The material was tougher and the two brothers argued with one another over the proper procedure. Her panties, stained and smelling of her unwashed body were the easiest.

At last she stood before them, somewhat ashamed of the bruises and cuts in her skin, intensely conscious of the dirt and smell of her unwashed person, overall pleased at the attention that her thin wiry body elicited from the two men. They held her at arms' length for a second, both pairs of male eyes examining her. She knew she smelled, and was surprised and gratified when the two of them hugged her in a triple embrace, then knelt in turn to kiss her pussy. Her juices started welling up within her at that moment, and gradually, as the evening wore on she forgot about her concerns, and about the coming attack.

The bath was the most beautiful Hanako had seen in a long time. The large picture window looked out upon a small formal garden. Bottles of lotions and soaps, many of them with the Clouds and Rain trademark, lined a well equipped set of shelves above the bath.

Jim and Andy made her squat on one of the sweet-smelling cedar-wood stools. For the first time in her life she found men attending to her body the way she had often attended to theirs. Jim and Andy soaped her from head to foot, taking particular care of the inner part of her thighs. She raised her buttocks obligingly for Andy, recalling his preferences, and was delighted to find his soapy finger delicately cleaning her rear hole. The smile on his face indicated promises of things to come. Then both men shampooed her hair, rubbing her scalp briskly with their fingers. They both had to stand near her face while doing so, and Omi, feeling braver and wanting to show her appreciation for their attentions, examined the two heavily swinging pricks with her eyes and tongue. The two cocks were as similar as the rest of her two lovers' parts. Except for the fact that Jim's was slightly darker, she thought they could have been twins. Shyly at first, then with growing confidence she flicked her tongue at the two organs. They responded appreciatively by growing in front of her eyes.

When she sucked in first one then the other of the two erections someone chuckled over her head and remarked that at that rate they would not be able to finish the shampoo properly. Abashed, she drew back, only to realize the remark was not serious when another prick bobbed purposefully near her lips.

They rinsed her off with hot water, then gravely helped her into the tub. She sank deeply into the hot water, sighing gratefully as she did so, her body totally relaxed. She watched with interest as the two men soaped themselves. Their erections softened somewhat, only to rise again as they soaped the curls at their crotches and deliberately frigged the thick male poles. Both cocks were jutting forward and upwards as Jim and Andy climbed into the bath and sank gratefully into the steaming waters.

They crowded together, the clean hot water rising to their chins. Hanako felt their hands on her, stroking her body under the surface. She reciprocated by rubbing the two erect poles under water. First one, then the other kissed her deeply, and the hands on her breasts came from two different bodies. She found a foot between her legs and maneuvered herself over it. Whoever it was recognized her intention and she found herself soon being frigged by someone's large toe. Another hand, disappointed that her cunt was occupied, found solace in the crack of her ass. The kisses on her neck and mouth turned more insistent and demanding. She reciprocated as well as she could, but soon was wanting more than the bath. She rose slowly, water streaming from her slim form. This time Jim and Andy looked on appreciatively as she posed before them. They hurried out of the bath themselves, and amidst her protests and attempts to fight back dried her with one of the unusually fluffy towels.

Someone had set out a large double *futon* in a room near the bath. They lay down on it together. She turned to them but Jim stopped her with an upraised palm. From the sleeve of his sleeping *nemaki* robe he produced a small bottle. Andy grinned at the sight of the bottle. They poured some of the straw-coloured viscous liquid onto her skin and began rubbing it in. It smelled of flowers, but also of musk and other things. Soon the pheromone started doing its thing. The twins were hard put to hold the girl down. Hanako mewled with frustration, reaching blindly for male cocks and for her own flowering sex. They turned her over onto her stomach and rubbed her back, her buttocks, the nape of her neck. Gradually the heat in Hanako's loins grew stronger. She tried to clench her legs and rub her thighs together, she tried to grasp one of the elusive cocks she could see out of the corner of her eyes. Her body writhed in the throes of instant mindless lust. Her nipples were as hard and erect as the men's cocks. A finger insinuated itself between her cunt lips, stroked briefly then withdrew. She exploded in an orgasm that only banked the internal fires while it was going on, then blew them up again, ready for another one. This time the intruder was someone's tongue, while hands held her legs apart. Again she exploded, the ripples of her orgasm coursing through her wiry body. Fingers again, this time on her breasts, and her body arced to meet them.

After six or seven small intense orgasms the sensitivity of her flesh passed and she found she could think coherently again. The climaxes had not exhausted her resources, instead they had left her with an intense deep lust for the two men lying beside her. Jim offered a drink of water and Andy grabbed the glass away. He filled his mouth, leaned over her and trickled the fluid into her parched throat. She drank thirstily and greedily, then sucked at his tongue for dessert. Jim's mouth followed until she had drunk her fill. They stroked her skin again. It was rough in some spots, covered by the scars of outdoor living. They kissed her body, readying her for them.

Hanako raised her head. "I want both of you," she said.

Jim was the first to respond. He knelt between her legs, spreading them wide. His cock jutted forward and up and he had difficulty forcing the head down to her waiting entrance. The tiny lips seemed to grasp the head and Hanako arched her body high and cried out loud as the wide crown penetrated her. Jim tried to push further in and discovered it was not necessary. Hanako was forcing her hips onto him, her legs wide, her feet planted on the bedding. She shook her hips, her eyes closed, squeezing inexpertly at his cock with the muscles of her cunt. Andy watched for a while, then began rubbing her prominently erect clitoris with one hand while squeezing her breast with the other. Jim clutched her ass and helped her establish a rhythm, his groping hands causing greater friction against his own cock.

Hanako's belly muscles started rippling. Cries came from her, silenced every once in a while as she sought Andy's mouth, tonguing him forcefully. She sought both men with her hands, anxiously gripping their muscles and pulling at their arms as if afraid they were going to escape. With one last convulsive heave Jim found his essence being sucked out of him. He groaned, his jaws clenched and raised skywards as an electric flow was forced out of him. Hanako gave one final muted scream, then collapsed, pulling both men to her.

Jim and Hanako lay silently for a moment, both breathing heavily. Then Jim rolled off her. Andy looked at her questioningly. The radical student smiled and opened her legs.

"Once again," she said in a trembling voice. "I will never have enough."

Andy laughed joyously as he mounted her and she echoed his laughter. This time she locked legs behind the man's back and rubbed her hairy mound against him with abandon. She squeezed her own prominent brown nipples until Jim took over the task for her while Andy once again stuffed her mouth with his tongue. Her actions were just as frantic as before, as if she had not reached an orgasm minutes earlier. Her cries echoed in the small room and her sweat and the ointment raised a powerful musk. Jim rose suddenly. The ointment had affected him and Andy no less than Hanako, and by now he was as horny as he had been before. Andy raised his mouth from her lips and she opened her eyes to see Jim crouched before her face with an erect cock once again.

She released Andy's shoulders and reached for the erection. For a long delicious moment she stroked the hard virile member, still moving her hips in a blind fiery lust, then she brought it to her lips. The crown slipped onto her tongue and her eyes closed again as she sucked more of the shaft in, her head supported by Jim's hands. He pulled out of her mouth and she sucked at the receding shaft with disappointment. The shelf below the tip caught on her lips and she sucked again, energetically. Jim knelt again, behind her head this time. She tilted her head backwards until she could see his balls hanging down in front of her face, swelling and receding rhythmically. Above it jutted his horn, dark and purple tipped. Andy looked on with interest, still shafting her cunt hole with all the energy he could muster. Hanako mewled again with frustration, unable to muster the patience for the delightful inevitable. Jim split his knees apart until the shaft lay over her lips. Unable to reach the tip and insert it, Hanako busily licked the shaft. Jim leaned forward and held her heels, pulling them high over Andy's back and exposing her mound more fully to his brother's thrusts. She moaned again, her tongue licking at Jim's hairy balls. The position was uncomfortable, but delightful all the same as Andy's engorged prick found its way deeper into her.

Jim slid back and poised the tip of his cock before her lips. She knew what she had to do, wanted to do. The head of the male shaft, smelling of their intermingled juices slid forward. She flattened her tongue against the bottom side of the shaft and was rewarded by a groan from Jim. Slowly he eased forward. At first she was afraid of gagging, but the discipline she had learned in the commune and exercised for the benefit of the Committee for Capitalist Eradication stood her in good stead. The beautiful fleshy shaft slid through her mouth and probed at her throat. By an effort of pure will she relaxed the muscles at her glottis and was rewarded by the feel of the large living morsel sliding down her throat.

Jim almost shot his entire load as he reached Hanako's throat. The feel of the corrugations of her membranes were a completely new sensation. He revelled in the touch of her nose against his balls, which he could feel distinctly, and peering down he saw her chin butting against his black pubic hair. Carefully he withdrew so that the tip of his cock rested in her mouth. She breathed easily, licking and sucking at the tip of the shaft, then urged him in by the simple expedient of clutching at his buttocks and pulling. He responded by pushing in again.

The feel of the long shaft fucking her throat was exquisite. Andy too was suiting his motions to the speed of his brother's. The two cocks, one at either end, started moving together in a slow and easy cadence, pausing at each withdrawal, then slowing and inexorably sliding into her again. The eagerness of the previous fuck had passed, though its intensity had not diminished. She let the men fuck her slowly, her own lust growing with every movement. Finally there came a moment when she had to have it all. One of her hands clenched at the bunched muscles above her head. The other pulled at the hips driving the shaft into her cunt. She quivered mightily, unable to truly move. Her insides shuddered and the spasms infected the two men. They quivered as well, and throughout her own powerful orgasm she was conscious of the flood of semen that rushed down her throat and up her vagina to damp though not quench the fire in her belly.

They rested for a while, Andy pouring them all some tea. Idle talk was punctuated by idle stroking. She told them of her life in the commune, and of the Committee's plans. Neither seemed worried. Instead, they started taking a greater interest in her, their hands stroking her flanks and breasts, their mouths, still hot from the tea, warming her nipples. The banked fire in her loins rose again. Andy was behind her as she turned to kiss Jim, stroking her narrow behind. She thought she could recall his preferences, and his choice pleased her. Rolling onto her stomach, her mouth in Jim's crotch, her lips rousing his erection, she said into the black thicket, "Fuck me from behind," and spread her legs.

Andy knelt behind her and spread her buns. They were slick with sweat and he exposed the tiny bud of her asshole, then opened her cunt as well. The lips parted readily, the remains of his plentiful residue dripping from between them. He aimed his shaft at the tiny rear hole and inserted the tip. Hanako was tight, almost virginal. The ring muscles parted reluctantly as he squeezed into them, watching the flanges at the head of his cock distend the tissue.

"Wait!" she commanded as the anal muscles started closing over his shaft. Jim was in full erection and she examined her mouth's work critically. She came to her knees slowly so as not to dislodge the wonderful knob in her ass. Jim saw her look and did not have to be told what to do. He slid under her, his legs projecting between Andy's. Holding his shaft erect he watched as Hanako lowered herself, fitting the tiny lips of her cunt around the purple tip of his shaft.

"Together," she gasped, and a long wail of delight left her mouth as Jim and Andy shoved their cocks into her.

The three of them rested thus for a long time, joined together at their roots. Hanako raised her head to Andy and kissed the side of his mouth. Crouched above her he inserted his tongue as deeply as he could. Beneath them Jim raised his head and seized one of her nipples, sucking it in deeply, then pulling with his teeth. She released Andy and bent forward to Jim's waiting mouth. They kissed as Andy squeezed her breasts and nibbled at her scarred shoulder.

"Now fuck me, hard!" she commanded.

Her screams were the unabashed expression of her joy as the male hips thrust their precious loads into her waiting cunt and backside. They went on for a long time as the cool wind blew down from the mountains and moaned counterpoint in the pine trees.

# CHAPTER 16:

# RED FLAGS IN THE MORNING

Numajiri looked at his group. They were as ready as they ever would be. He saw Ito's eyes focused on him. "Do you think she'll do it?" he asked rhetorically. More than Omi were on trial here, and Ito knew that.

"She will," he said confidently.

Numajiri grinned a death's head grin. "Good, then we'll have a martyr to the cause."

The pre-dawn breeze was blowing from the castle to the forest. All the better, he thought. The capitalist lackeys were unlikely to have guard dogs, but there was always a chance, and they needed every edge. He was pleased with himself. The team was a good one, and he was glad to have the chance to lead them. This assault would show the world that the Radical Red Front: Central Faction was not to be trifled with. *And* they would be disposing of both running dogs and backsliders such as Omi. She had been displaying obvious signs of disaffection for the past six months her commune leader had told Numajiri.

He looked about him with a great deal of pride. Much depended on the success of this raid. They would be able to show they were more prominent than their rivals from the Red Army, and they would also garner support and recruits. That was what they needed, Numajiri thought. More recruits, such as Maki who was sitting at his side. He had never before noted how truly committed she was, how, in fact, she enhanced every meeting she was in, notwithstanding her constant carping on ideological purity. In fact, he thought, she is a remarkably handsome woman, a true benefit to the cause.

He noticed that the knees of her camouflage paint-splashed jeans were torn and he pointed it out to her silently as Ito went over their assignments. The smooth touch of her skin electrified him. It obviously affected her as well. Her snub-nosed face looked at the hand on her knee, then at Numajiri's face, and finally at the bulge in his pants. Deliberately and without haste she unzipped his fly while Ito stopped speaking and Akabane, the head of the Star Group who lead the assault, discussed the ideological purity of their mission. Numajiri's stubby thick cock sprang into the cool pre-dawn air. Maki stared at it for a short while, as if not certain what to do, then undid the buttons of her own pants and raised her bottom from the ground. The pants slid off. She wore no underwear and Numajiri caught a glimpse of dark crotch hairs before she squirmed around and presented her pale buttocks to his lap.

She was wet and ready as she impaled herself. Akabane's exhortations to do their best were answered as she sat forcefully into Numajiri's lap. She watched the rest of the group. Ito looked at her, as did the others except

Tsukuda. She had risen to her feet a look of horror on her face. Akabane turned to look at her. His head turned slowly, as if he fought against some massive current. Then he was on his feet beside her. He stroked her full flank. She had tiny breasts and broad peasant hips and thighs which she often concealed by wearing baggy clothes. Maki had been aware of this tendency of hers to be concerned with personal appearance, and had reprimanded her for bourgeois backsliding several times. Now Maki watched as Akabane placed another hand on her breast. Tsukuda started to object, then seemed to think the better of it.

That was the last Maki saw of Tsukuda for some time. Ito was standing before her, hiding the sight. His long thin cock was erect and pointed at her out of the gaping front of his fly. She held the long stick in one hand examining it curiously. Though he had poked her a number of times—it was the duty of members to share everything and Maki took her duties seriously—she had never actually seen his cock, much less held it. Their couplings had always been brisk, interludes as it were, between discussions of ideology and tactics. The crown was rather small for the shaft, and the tip was already wet with his preliminary discharge. She poised the spongy-hard stick at her mouth and he pushed out his hips. Maki sucked him in, oooing her lips. Ito grunted and pushed forward relentlessly. Only her fist on the shaft saved her from having to swallow him whole. In the meantime, the movement of her ass on Numajiri's lap had not ceased. His hands were now on her hips, urging her soft buns down onto his crotch. With each movement he grunted as her weight pushed the air out of his lungs.

Maki felt another figure squatting by her side. It was Goto, whom everyone called Dwarf. His long apelike arms were stretched out and soon she felt his hand on her breasts. The touch of his work-roughened fingers excited her to a fever pitch and he began pinching and twisting her nearer nipple. Out of the corner of her eye she caught sight of Fujii. His long hair framed his face as he bent from considerable height to observe the four on the ground. His cock—surprisingly small for such a tall man—was out, and he was masturbating furiously. With her free left hand Maki obliged him, helping him stroke his hard flesh. He straightened up again, and let their joined hands stroke him to full tumescence. Maki pulled him closer, first rubbing the shaft against her bobbing cheek, then spitting out Ito's stick, she hurriedly gave a few quick sucks to Fujii. An idea occurred to her and forced both men closer, then widened her mouth as much as she could. With some effort she managed to fit the tips of both cocks into her mouth from either side. Then she proceeded to lick and suck at both crowns simultaneously. She was intrigued by the difference in taste and smell between the two cocks, and as her lustful excitement grew, she would take both sticks out and rub them violently over her face.

When she had felt the wetness in her groin, Tsukuda knew there was something wrong. Excitement always gripped her before action. Joining the radical Center group had been the most exciting thing in her boring existence, and action was the apex of that feeling. The fact that her parents—part-time farmers—disapproved, made it all the more delicious. But she had never experienced excitement such as this. Her loins had never glowed before, nor the nipples on her tiny breasts ever swelled so much they were almost painful. She was conscious of the bulges in the men's pants as she had never been before. She stood up automatically, thinking to go deeper into the dark forest, when Akabane, the handsome young leader of the Star group, had risen to stand by her. She had had sex with him many times, so she was not particularly shaken by his hand on her haunch (though what Maki, that purist would say, was unpleasantly anticipated). It was when Akabane kissed her that shock completely overcame her. She had fucked with all the members of the group, as was only right. She had had that explained to her the first time she had joined the group. Forcefully. But she had never allowed them to kiss her, and the pleasure from the act was more a release from tension than really enjoyable. Now she felt herself responding to the demands of his tongue. Her own mouth opened involuntarily and she explored his tongue with her own. Her hands rose, stroked along his powerful muscular shoulders, and ended around his neck. Other hands joined his on her hips. From one side Yamaguchi pulled at her jeans. Takagi opened the zipper, and together he and Yamaguchi slid the pants down her heavy muscular legs and calves.

Then a most extraordinary thing happened. Takagi spread her legs and she found herself being kissed by two men. Takagi was the more skilled of the two. The touch of his tongue on her pussy made her grind her hips against the man and at the same time urged her mouth more deeply onto Akabane who was kissing her mouth. The electrifying sensations went on. She cried out, then again as Yamaguchi's hands squeezed between her body and Akabane's and started squeezing her flat breasts. Within seconds she was trembling so hard that only the pressure of the men's bodies was keeping her erect. The trembling grew stronger, and waves of a pleasure she had never felt before started rising from her groin. She urged her men on, faster and faster, whining into Akabane's searching mouth and grinding her body at the touches of the other two men. Her nerves were tingling and her body jerked convulsively. She gave a loud cry, clutching at all the males around her, then felt a sudden beautiful wave of release speed through her body. She was barely conscious of her surroundings as she jerked again and again against Takagi's mouth, then subsided into Akabane's strong arms. Without opening her eyes she was conscious of being born backwards, someone spreading a poncho on the ground, of the head disappearing from between her thighs and of her thighs being spread apart. But she was conscious of the wonderful warm penis that was inserted between her cunt lips and deep into her vagina, just as she was conscious of the hands that held her wide hips. When the steamy knob of a cock was presented to her mouth she gulped at it with as much glee and relief as the mouth that was now fastened over one of her nipples.

In the mansion overlooking the forest, Jim and Andy stared unbelievingly at the scene enacted by the members of the Committee for Capitalist Eradication. Between them, her hands in their laps, Hanako looked on with interest not unmingled with pleasure at her former comrades fall from ideological grace.

"Not bad, these thermal scopes," Kitamura said to Fine. Six of them were assembled in a comfortable sitting room. Before them four large screens showed the doings in the clearing below. The remotes, whose former quiet movement as they sneaked through the forest had made Andy seasick, were stationary now. And the pictures coming through from each camera were perfectly clear and detailed.

Mayumi was sitting next to the two older men, before a complicated console. She too had been looking on avidly, though her eyes flicked occasionally to Jim and Andy, whom she could see in profile.

"Mayumi," Fine turned to her and caught her examination of the two young men. He winked, jerked his head in their direction while saying, "Let the assault group go in now."

She smiled, nodded, whispered into her throat mike, then moved her chair closer to Jim. Her shoeless foot, clad in thin nylons, rose and began stroking his shoulder lightly.

Several figures slid into the clearing. The attackers were composed of both men and women. They were lithe and quick, and quite naked but for black thick-soled *tabi* socks. They attacked with silent intensity, and were in the middle of the Committee before the radicals knew what was happening.

Maki learned of the attack only when she found herself pulled off Numajiri's sperm sodden prick and laid gently but forcefully on the ground. Her mouth was filled with the first rush of Ito's come which she did not know whether to spit out or swallow. A man she had never seen before was mounting her. His cock was firmly erect and perfectly delicious. She gave herself over to the pleasure of his hands and lips, and most importantly, his cock. His hands slid over her skin like liquid fire, and her pleasure rose to a pitch she had never felt before. She turned her head slightly at a high wailing sound. It came from Fujii. He was inserted fully between the plump buttocks of a female black-socked attacker, and another had her head between his legs where she was licking and nibbling furiously. Beside her, his jerking foot coming into trip-hammer contact with her body she could hear Goto the Dwarf snorting as he fucked furiously at the willing body of another attacker. The raider had her heels locked over Goto's sweating back and she was urging him on with cries that matched his own and with claws that dug deep red scratches into his back.

Numajiri and Ito reacted violently to the attacker's presence. Numajiri had just spurted the last drops of his load into Maki's willing cunt. His cock was still hard and she was pleasantly expecting another orgasm that was building up inexorably in his balls, when Maki was hauled roughly off him. He leaped to his feet, cock quivering before him and searched frantically for his favorite weapon, a five foot iron pipe loaded with lead. A figure faced him. He charged forward screaming. The female figure, completely nude, danced away in the dark. But a hand slid down his back and pulled down his pants. He tripped and fell. Reflexes from years in the underground helped him roll away from an expected counterattack. He managed to rise, slipping out of his pants as he did so. The figure attacked. Cool soft fingers stroked his chest leaving a trail of delightful, stultifying fire. Another soft hand stroked the length of his still-aroused cock. He struck with the edge of his hand. The woman attacker swayed back, then pressed her soft chest to his side, rubbing taut nipples at his skin. She tripped him, and they fell together, tumbling on the cold pine needles. He sought for her throat and she avoided him. He was conscious that she was straddling him, her moist cunt searching actively for his erection. Instinctively his aroused body reacted to the presence of a female. He thrust upwards. His cock slid into a warm moist interior and he knew he had lost. Still fighting on he managed to fasten his hands around her neck. She tensed the tendons and he lost precious time searching for her windpipe. By the time he had found it, her mouth was breathing into his. His body overwhelmed his political convictions and he found himself searching hungrily for her mouth and his hips jerked into hers.

Ito was in the process of spurting into Maki's mouth, something he had never done before except in his imagination. Bourgeois emphasis on sex and its variations was looked down upon in the Commune. He stood there, paralyzed by his own spasming balls, as the attackers filled the clearing. He whirled to reach for a weapon. Before him a female figure was in the act of kneeling. He checked his rush. His glasses had fogged from his efforts in Maki's mouth, and he was not sure just *what* was facing him. She rose on her knees and captured his still dripping cock in her mouth. The pleasure was so intense Ito stopped his movements as if poleaxed. Maki's barely educated mouth was nothing like that, and he soon found himself jerking again and again into the exploring mouth that held him in velvet vise, one he had no intention of escaping from.

Tsukuda was well into her second orgasm. Takagi was between her legs and he proved to be a much more skillful lover than Akabane, who was squatting by her side as an interested observer, had ever been. She hazily considered the fact that he might have been dissembling, hiding his ability in sex so as not to arouse ire of others in the group. Just now, however, she was enjoying the sensation of his *suribachi* movement as he deliberately and with growing speed ground his cock into her, touching all sides of her cunt and mound with his circular movements. She cried out, not even trying to restrain her emotions this time as a flood of pleasure washed through her. They clutched at one another and Tsukuda closed her eyes. Flashes of lightning seemed to go off behind her lids. Then she reluctantly released Takagi's body as he rose off her. She was surprised and more than gratified to have his weight replaced by another. She opened her eyes, expecting Yamaguchi, and finding a stranger. She wanted to scream, to object, then thought the better of it. The stranger, who was grinning into her face in the growing light of dawn, was even better than Takagi had been. Several other strangers were around. Two were crouching by her, assisting the man whose cock was churning up a storm of pleasure in her insides. Takagi and Yamaguchi were wrapped into a knot with a strange woman. Akabane was nowhere to be seen in the dimness, but from the sounds around her, Tsukuda assumed he was involved in much the same thing all the others were. Thought lifted from her mind and she concentrated·solely on her own pleasure, on the searching hands and mouths, on the demanding cocks. She rolled over willingly when these demands became insistent and was completely relaxed when hard, divine cocks were pressed to her lips and tiny rear entrance. She gasped once, with the pleasure of it all, as the three strangers started moving into her at once.

"How the hell did they do that?" Andy whispered, half to himself, half to the other viewers.

"Look at that, they just overcame them. . . ." Jim was leaning forward, intent on the four scenes before them. None of the Committee members had managed to land a blow. Every stroke and nibble and nudge of the attackers had countered the violence with pleasure, and all of the Committee members were currently too busy to entertain thoughts of violence. Or any thoughts at all, for that matter, as their bodies were manipulated in erotic ways they would not have imagined earlier.

"You've heard of Judo? *Kendo?*" Kitamura was speaking. "Well, there are a lot of other martial arts. This one is perhaps the most esoteric of all. It was developed by a Buddhist order of nuns originating in the Dosojin-in nunnery in these mountains. It was suppressed by the Tokugawa shoguns: too dangerous to the public order, they thought. I discovered traces of it and together with Lenny have developed and refined it." He grinned and his glasses twinkled in the light of the scopes. "Lenny's chemicals help a lot, too. We let off pheromone bombs in the lower garden and the wind did the rest.''

''They're not listening,'' Leaonard Fine whispered with a grin. Kitamura turned from the screen. Hanako's legs were resting on Jim and Andy's knees and their hands had disappeared inside the light kimono she wore. Mayumi was leaning over them. Her blouse open and her breasts had tumbled out of the white lace of her petticoat. Jim's hand was sliding up her nyloned leg and disappearing beneath her skirt.

''Time for two old men like us to go,'' Kitamura said approvingly. He stared approvingly at their children.

''Yes,'' Fine answered grinning. ''There are several lab assistants we could interview.''

Their tiptoed exit was unnecessary. The four on the couch would have paid no attention to a brass band.

# ◖BLUE MOON BOOKS